Heartland™

Tomorrow's Promise

Lauren Brooke

■SCHOLASTIC

With special thanks to Linda Chapman

*To Linda Tellington-Jones, who first developed T-touch.
Her books are inspirational, and have helped people
to understand horses in a new and enlightened way.*

Scholastic Children's Books,
Euston House, 24 Eversholt Street,
London NW1 1DB, UK
a division of Scholastic Ltd
London ~ New York ~ Toronto ~ Sydney ~ Auckland
Mexico City ~ New Delhi ~ Hong Kong

First published in the UK by Scholastic Ltd, 2003
Series created by Working Partners Ltd

10 digit ISBN 0 439 98193 X
13 digit ISBN 978 0439 98193 4

Typeset by TW Typesetting, Midsomer Norton, Somerset
Printed and bound in Denmark by Nørhaven Paperback A/S, Viborg

8 10 9 7

Chapter One

Dark patches of sweat stood out on the bay gelding's coat. He snorted loudly, his eyes darting around the bustling showground. Lifting up a hoof, he struck out violently at the grass.

"Gerry!" exclaimed Hannah Boswell, his rider.

Snatching at the reins, the bay reared in excitement. Struggling to bring him under control, Hannah turned him in a tight circle, almost knocking over a tall, slim girl who was watching.

"Sorry, Amy," Hannah gasped. "He gets really excited when he's about to go into the ring."

"Easy, boy," Amy Fleming said in a low and soothing voice. Moving in beside the horse's head, she put her hand on his warm neck and began to move his skin in light circles. The gelding blew at her. "Hush, Spartan," Amy whispered. She caught herself quickly, hoping that Hannah hadn't noticed. *Not Spartan*, she thought. *He's Gerry now.*

But in her mind, Amy knew that he would always be Spartan – the beautiful horse who had come to her family's equine sanctuary almost a year ago, after being involved in a terrible road accident. It had turned out that he had been stolen. At Heartland, Amy had helped him recover from the trauma of the accident, and had finally reunited him with his old owners – Hannah's family.

Amy's fingers worked on the bay gelding's neck and gradually the tension seemed to leave his body. He breathed out deeply and nudged her gently with his nose.

Hannah watched Amy in wonderment. "How did you do that?"

Amy shrugged. "It's just something my mom taught me." She patted the now-calm gelding. "Crazy animal," she said affectionately. "If you went into the ring as excited as that you'd knock the fences flying."

"That's true," Hannah said ruefully. "He's knocked a fence down in the jump-off in the last three shows. He gets so psyched up."

"You could try massaging some diluted lavender oil around his nostrils before you tack him up," said Amy. "It's very relaxing. And adding scullcap and valerian powder to his feed for a few days before each show should help."

"Really?" Hannah said. "OK, I'll try that." She looked at

Amy. "I can't believe you know all this stuff. Did your —" she hesitated — "did your mom teach it all to you?"

Amy understood Hannah's hesitation. Her mom had been killed in the road accident that had left Spartan traumatized. After rescuing him from an abandoned barn, they had been taking him back to Heartland when a storm had blown up and a tree had fallen on the trailer. "Yes, she taught me everything," Amy said quietly.

The loudspeaker suddenly crackled into life. "And now for the jump-off for Class 146 — The Marshall and Sterling Children's Jumper Classic. We begin with number 203, owner and rider, Hannah Boswell, riding Dancing Grass Geronimo."

The steward started to open the in-gate. Hannah tightened her reins.

"Go for it, Hannah!" Amy called.

"Just watch us!" Hannah replied.

Amy hurried to the stands. Sinking down on a seat, she pushed her long light-brown hair back from her face and watched intently as Gerry cantered into the ring. He looked keen but controlled, his coat gleaming like dark oak in the bright sun. The shortened course of six jumps looked high but inviting. It was timed, which meant the horse that jumped the fastest with the least faults would win.

As the starting buzzer went, a thought flashed through Amy's mind. *I could be riding him now if he were still at Heartland.* A pang of regret shot through her, but as horse and rider reached the first fence the idea was forgotten.

"Come on, boy," she breathed, sliding to the edge of her seat. Gerry's stride lengthened and he soared over the first fence. Amy's upper body moved forward as if she were jumping with him.

Careful now, don't go too fast or you'll have one down, she thought as Hannah turned towards the next fence. Gerry speeded up in excitement. But Hannah was ready. Sitting back, she set him up perfectly. Gerry's forelegs snapped tight to his chest. The brush fence, the in-and-out, the triple, the wall. He cleared them all with inches to spare.

Amy let out a huge sigh as he galloped through the finish. He was clear and his time was fast. Jumping to her feet, she hurried out of the stand. "Way to go!" she yelled to Hannah.

"Wasn't he great?" Hannah gasped, patting Gerry's neck as if she was never going to stop.

"The best," Amy agreed.

"I'm so lucky to have him," Hannah said, her blue eyes shining. "He is just so special."

As if he understood what she was saying, Gerry turned and nuzzled Hannah's leg. The happiness in his eyes was obvious.

"I'd better walk him around to cool him off," Hannah said to Amy. She dismounted. "There's not much I can do now but wait and see how the others in the class go."

Amy nodded and fell into step beside her.

"So, why aren't you competing today?" Hannah asked curiously. "Where's Sundance?"

"He pulled a tendon last week," Amy explained. "Our vet,

Scott, said he can't be ridden for at least three months."

"Nightmare," Hannah said, shocked.

"I know," Amy replied. She forced a smile. "Still, Sundance thinks it's OK. He's getting totally spoilt."

"Not so good for you though," Hannah said sympathetically. "You won't get to show this summer at all."

Amy shook her head. "Well, we're so busy at Heartland at the moment that I probably wouldn't have had the time anyway." She spoke positively, but she couldn't help feeling a bit down. Helping damaged horses would always come first with her, but, once in a while, it was great to ride a horse that didn't need her help. She loved taking Sundance to shows when she got the chance.

Trying to hide her disappointment, she patted Gerry's damp shoulder. "I'm getting a soda," she said to Hannah. "Do you want one?"

"Thanks." Hannah smiled at Amy. "You know, I'm really glad you're here," she said. "My grandparents couldn't make it. Chuck — Grandpa's head-groom — drove me down, but he's watching the hunters. It's good to have someone rooting for me."

Amy smiled back. *I wish Hannah lived closer*, she thought as she headed across the busy showground. *We could see more of each other then — maybe even go to shows together*. Amy caught herself. She had to stop thinking like that. She wasn't going to compete at shows again. Next year she'd be too big for Sundance. She just had to accept it.

She found the food tent, and bought two cans of soda. She was hurrying back to Hannah when a rider on a flashy chestnut trotted straight into her path. Amy stepped back just in time. "Hey!"

As the rider reined in her horse, Amy saw that it was Ashley Grant. Ashley's parents had a show barn near to Heartland called Green Briar, where they trained push-button show horses and ponies using force and strict discipline. Ashley and Amy attended the same high school, but that was all they had in common.

Ashley smirked at Amy. "I see you couldn't face the competition in the Large Pony Hunter then, Amy?" she said.

"Sundance is lame," Amy said curtly.

Ashley shook her head. "You know, it's a real shame you haven't got a better animal. You used to be quite good." Smugly, she patted the chestnut's neck. "So what do you think of Bright Magic? He's a Danish Warmblood."

Amy looked at the chestnut. About sixteen hands high, with four white socks, he was beautiful.

"He's worth well over five figures," Ashley said. "I'm competing him in Junior Jumpers. Mom thought it was time I moved out of ponies, now that I'm almost sixteen. So even when Sundance gets over his lameness, we won't be competing against each other. I'm moving into the big time, Amy." A smile curved across Ashley's beautiful face. "Shame you're not going to be there to be beaten into second place."

Amy looked at Ashley in disgust. "You just don't get it, do

you, Ashley? I don't ride just to win prizes, and I don't care how much a horse is worth."

But Ashley wasn't listening. She was staring at something over Amy's shoulder. "Would you look at that!" she said incredulously.

Amy looked round. A strawberry roan mare was being ridden towards the warm-up ring. Her head was coarse and her legs stocky as a carthorse's. Her dark-haired rider was slightly built. Amy guessed he was about eighteen. His riding jacket was patched at the elbows and his tan breeches had obviously seen better days. Even Amy couldn't help but stare. Next to the other entrants, this horse and rider looked totally out of place.

"Hey, you!" Ashley called out to the boy. "You on the roan!" Her clear voice rang out across the ground.

The boy turned, his eyes taking in Ashley on her horse and Amy standing beside her. "Me?" he said, his forehead creasing into a frown.

"Yes, you," Ashley said, rolling her eyes as if to say who else could she be speaking to. "What classes are you entered for?"

"The Open Jumping and the Six Bar," the boy answered shortly.

Amy felt her eyes widening. Only the best horses competed in those classes.

Ashley raised her eyebrows disbelievingly. "Yeah, right," she said. "So, what are you really entered for?"

"I told you," the boy repeated, his voice icy. "I'll be going into the Six Bar in a moment and the Open Jumping this afternoon." Glaring at her and Amy, he signalled to his horse to move on.

Ashley laughed. "I don't know who's worse – him or his carthorse!"

The boy swung round. It was clear from his face that he had heard her every word.

"Ashley!" A sharp voice behind them made the girls turn round. Val Grant, Ashley's mom, was marching towards them, her tanned forehead creased in a deep frown. "What are you doing, standing around like that? I thought I told you to work Magic!"

For a moment, Amy almost felt sorry for Ashley, but then she decided Ashley deserved everything she got. As Val Grant approached, Amy left to find Hannah.

Amy and Hannah watched the last few horses in the jump-off, fingers crossed in suspense.

"You did it!" Amy said excitedly as the final horse knocked down the first element of the triple. "You've won, Hannah!"

"I can't believe it!" Hannah cried.

The announcer called out the winner's number and, remounting, Hannah rode into the ring to collect the blue ribbon.

After horse and rider had been photographed, Amy walked back with them to the Dancing Grass trailer. There was a note from Chuck on the windscreen saying that he'd gone to watch the hunters in ring one and that Hannah should call him on his mobile when she was ready to leave.

Just then a voice coming over the loudspeaker announced that the Six Bar competition was about to start. "I'd really like to see that," Hannah said. "Do you want to watch it with me?"

Amy checked her watch. Ty was collecting her in an hour by the main gates. "Sure," she grinned. She loved watching Six Bar competitions, where the fences – six of them – were set out in a row across the ring, each one a few inches higher than the last. You had to jump all of them and any horse that jumped clear went through to the next round when the fences were raised another couple of inches. The fences kept going up and up until there was a winner. It was a real test of agility and power.

Amy and Hannah loaded Gerry into his trailer and hurried to the main jumping ring where they found two seats in the stands.

"And now for our next competitor, number 365, Brooksby Light, owned by the Travers Company and ridden by Andrew Ramone."

A dapple-grey thoroughbred came into the ring. "He looks a bit like Pegasus, the horse my dad used to showjump," Amy told Hannah. As she watched the horse canter a circle, she felt a wave of sadness. Pegasus, her dad's Olympic showjumping partner, had died last year. Amy still missed him, and a day rarely went by when she didn't pause at his field gate and look for a moment at the oak sapling that marked the spot where he was buried.

"Cool horse," someone said in front of Amy.

Amy glanced down, and saw that the comment came from a group of junior riders who regularly jumped on the circuit. Not surprisingly, Ashley was sitting in the middle of them.

"Way to go," one of the others commented as the dapple-grey cleared all six fences and was ridden out to the sound of applause.

"Our second clear round," the announcer said. "And now for number 278, Burning Amber, owned and ridden by Daniel Lawson."

The gate opened and Amy looked again. Cantering into the ring was the strawberry roan mare that she had seen in the warm-up area. After the last horse, the mare looked even plainer than ever.

"It's Daniel," said Hannah, as a murmur ran round the crowd.

"You know him?" Amy said.

Hannah nodded. "He lives near our farm. I've seen him at shows. Just watch. Amber's amazing!"

Ashley and her friends were laughing loudly at the strawberry roan.

Amy shook her head as she saw Daniel glare in their direction. Just because Amber didn't look as good as the other horses it didn't mean she wasn't able to jump. Amy could see the power and drive in the mare's short back and sloping hindquarters and there was no doubt about the keenness in her eyes. Scowling at Ashley and her friends, Amy found herself willing the roan mare on.

"Daniel got her at a sale," Hannah whispered as Amber cantered in a circle. "No one wanted her. He bought her for next to nothing and then he found out what a good jumper she was."

The starting buzzer went. The crowd fell into a hush. It felt as though everyone was tensed and waiting for some disaster to befall the rider and his strange-looking horse.

Daniel headed Amber towards the line of fences. Her powerful hindquarters thrust down and she was over the first effortlessly, then on to the next. She soared over the jumps, her large hooves tucked precisely up underneath her, her body rounding over the bars. And all the time, Daniel sat tight to the saddle, his fingers light on the reins, his body perfectly centred over her withers. As he guided her safely over the sixth and final fence, her hooves landed sweetly on the grass and the crowd burst into applause.

"I told you Amber was good!" Hannah shouted to Amy above the noise. Meanwhile Daniel gently slowed his horse down and rode out of the ring, a look of satisfaction on his face. "Daniel only started competing her two years ago, but he's already upgraded to Open. It looks like he's going to take her all the way to the top."

After watching such a display of jumping, Amy readily

agreed with Hannah, and by the time she had watched Amber clear the jumps in the next two rounds, she was sure Daniel and Amber would go far.

By the fourth round, there were just three horses left – Amber, the dapple-grey and a chestnut stallion ridden by international showjumper Nick Halliwell. Amy knew Nick well – last summer she'd cured one of his young horses of its fear of trailers and, under normal circumstances, she'd have been wanting him to win the class. But today she wanted Amber to win. She wasn't alone. The second Amber came into the ring, the audience exploded. Seemingly unfazed by the noise, the roan mare calmly pricked her ears and cantered obediently in a circle. The fences were much higher now, the final fence standing at six foot. The dapple-grey had knocked two down. Nick Halliwell had knocked one. If Amber and Daniel could go clear, then she would get the blue ribbon.

The starting buzzer went. Daniel turned Amber into the first fence. In three powerful strides she flew over it. Over the next and the next until they soared cleanly over the last jump.

The crowd erupted, jumping to their feet, clapping and cheering. Amber put her head down in a triumphant buck.

"Wasn't that brilliant?" Hannah said in delight.

Amy stood up, clapping loudly. "Unreal!"

The announcer called Daniel and Amber back in to collect the blue ribbon and a trophy. As the photographers gathered, Amber turned her head and affectionately nuzzled her owner's leg. Ignoring the calls to look at the cameras, Daniel bent forward to rub her forehead. Amy smiled at the obvious bond between horse and rider.

Hannah stretched and stood up. "I should get going."

Amy followed her out of the stand. As they passed the warm-up ring, she saw Nick Halliwell dismounting from his stallion. "Hold on a minute," Amy called to Hannah.

She ducked under the rope. Already three or four people had gathered around Nick, holding programmes out for him to sign. He stopped what he was doing when he saw Amy and smiled. "Amy! How're you doing?"

"I'm fine," Amy replied. "I just wanted to say well done."

"Well, we didn't get the blue ribbon, but this fella's still young," Nick said, patting the stallion's flanks as his groom led the horse away. "Did you see the guy who won?"

"Yeah," Amy said. "Wasn't he great?"

Nick nodded. "He sure was. And what a horse." He took off his hat. "I'm glad I've seen you," he said to Amy. "I was going to give you a call. One of my youngsters is playing up. He was fine when he was backed a few months ago, but he's become very resistant recently. Scott's checked him over and can't find anything wrong. I thought maybe you could take a look at him."

"Sure," Amy agreed.

"I'll be in touch," Nick replied, turning to sign programmes again.

Amy began to hurry back towards Hannah.

"Watch out!" a voice shouted angrily.

Amy stopped with a gasp. She'd been so busy thinking about what Nick Halliwell had just said that she hadn't seen the roan mare cantering out of the ring, and had almost walked straight into her path. Looking up, Amy saw Daniel Lawson glaring furiously at her as he pulled Amber up.

"Why don't you look where you're going?" he roared from Amber's back.

"I'm ... I'm sorry," Amy stammered.

"Do you think you own this place or something?" Daniel demanded. "You people make me sick."

"What?" Amy was completely taken aback.

"You and your stuck-up friends," he snapped. "Looking down your noses at other people. Laughing at people like me and horses like Amber."

"What? But..."

Scowling angrily, Daniel trotted Amber away. Amy was left staring after him.

Hannah came over. "What was all that about?"

"He just called me stuck-up!" Amy burst out in astonishment. "He accused me of laughing at him!"

Hannah stared. "Weird. He's not very friendly on the show-circuit at home but he's not normally rude."

"Well, he sure was just now," Amy said, frowning.

"Forget it," Hannah said. She glanced round. "I should go and find Chuck. How are you getting back to Heartland?"

"Ty's giving me a lift," Amy answered. She looked at her watch. "Speaking of which, I'd better move it. I'm supposed to be meeting him at the gates about now. See you, Hannah. Congratulations!"

"Bye!" Hannah called.

Amy raced to the main entrance just in time to see her boyfriend, Ty, pulling up in his pick-up. Seeing his familiar face scanning the crowd for her, Amy felt her heart turn a somersault. For years, Ty had been just like an older brother working at the farm with her, but a few months ago they had started dating, and now she felt as if a light switched on inside her whenever she saw him.

She jogged over. "Hi!" she said, scrambling into the pick-up. "I've had the best day. Hannah's been here with Gerry – they won the Children's Jumper Classic – and I saw Nick Halliwell – he says he might have a horse to send to us. And then there was this strawberry roan mare. She—"

"Amy," Ty interrupted her.

Amy suddenly realized that he was frowning. "What's up?" she asked in surprise.

"You've had a phonecall … from your father…"

Chapter Two

Amy stared as Ty filled in the details. "A horse!" she said. "What do you mean, he's bought us a horse?" Her mind was spinning. Was this for real? Until a visit a few months ago she and her sister, Lou, hadn't had any contact with their father for twelve years. Now Ty was saying that he had bought them a horse, and that it was arriving that afternoon. "Tell me everything," she said excitedly.

"All I know is that it's sixteen hands and a Warmblood gelding," Ty told her, turning the pick-up out of the show-ground. "Your dad only called a few hours ago. Lou and your grandpa were out so I talked to him. He said he's been over here on business looking for young sports horses to export to Australia, and that he's seen this horse and decided to buy it for you and Lou."

"But why?" Amy burst out. "Did he say?"

"No," Ty answered. "He was on his way to see a client and said he couldn't talk for long. He's going to phone again this evening."

Amy sank back in the seat. She and Lou were getting a horse. A horse that wouldn't have to be rehomed or go back to its owners like most of the other horses at Heartland. Excitement welled up in her, but at the same time, she couldn't help thinking *why?* After all, it wasn't as if they needed another horse at Heartland. She already had Sundance and Lou was scared of riding – she had been for twelve years, ever since the riding accident that had ended their father's showjumping career.

A thought struck Amy as she remembered how, during their father's recent visit, Lou had promised him that she would face her fear and start riding again. Well, maybe he had bought this horse for Lou. He was an experienced horseman. He must have realized that few of the horses at Heartland were reliable enough for a nervous rider. *Of course*, Amy thought, *that's it. It makes sense.*

"You're quiet," Ty said, looking at her curiously.

"I've just been thinking about why Daddy's bought us this horse," Amy answered. "I figure it's for Lou. It'll be a reliable, quiet horse that she can get her confidence back on."

"Could be," Ty said thoughtfully.

"I bet I'm right," Amy said convinced. "I wonder what it's like. How old? What colour?" A grin spread across her face.

What did the details matter? It was a horse of their own — and it was coming to Heartland that afternoon. What could be better than that?

As Ty drove up Heartland's long drive, the white weather-boarded farmhouse and front stable block came into view. Amy saw Lou walking towards the house.

Hearing the pick-up, Lou stopped and shaded her eyes. Seeing it was Amy and Ty, she waved.

"Lou!" Amy exclaimed, throwing open the door as soon as Ty had parked. "Ty's told me about the horse."

"Can you believe it?" Lou said, looking almost put-out. "Apparently Daddy bought it on an impulse." She ran a hand through her short golden hair. "An impulse! How can anyone possibly just buy a horse on an impulse?"

Amy knew the answer to that, but she guessed that Lou, ever practical, might never understand.

"I mean, it's not as if we need another horse here," Lou went on. "We're busy enough as it is."

Amy followed Lou into the house. Jack Bartlett, their grandfather, was mending a broken halter at the kitchen table, his grey head bent over the leather. "I gather you've heard the news then," he said, looking up and taking in Amy's excited face.

"Yeah," Amy said. "Isn't it great?"

The creases in Grandpa's weather-beaten face deepened. "I'm not so sure, honey. If we use one of the stalls for this horse, it'll mean we've got one less for the horses who really need Heartland's help." He rubbed his forehead. "I'm sure your father means well, but I wish he'd asked first."

"Daddy's just so impractical," Lou said.

Amy felt stung. "Don't be so mean, Lou. After all, I reckon Daddy's bought this horse mainly for you."

A frown crossed Lou's face. "For me?"

"Well, it's not like I need a horse," Amy pointed out. "I've got all the others to ride. I think this horse is going to be a schoolmaster for you to learn to ride on again."

Lou looked stunned. "Gosh," she said. "Do you really think so?"

"Yes," Amy replied. She saw a look of wonder enter Lou's blue eyes.

"Well, I have been meaning to start riding again," Lou said thoughtfully, "but I've put it off because I didn't want to upset any of the horses here with my nerves. It would be different if we had a horse who was completely sensible."

"It'll be perfect, Lou," Amy enthused. "I'll help you. We can go for rides together."

"Now don't start making too many plans," Jack put in hastily. "We don't know anything definite about this horse yet."

"No," Amy said, grinning at Lou. "But I sure can't wait to find out!"

* * *

Leaving Grandpa and Lou in the kitchen, Amy went up the yard to get on with the chores. She thought about the imminent arrival. In her mind's eye she saw a bright bay with a noble head and kind eye – perfect for Lou to ride. It would probably be about twelve years old, still in its prime, but past the stage of being headstrong.

Amy remembered the look of surprise and happiness on Lou's face when she had told her that the horse must be for her. Although her sister had never said anything directly, Amy was sure that Lou thought their father preferred Amy to her. Amy knew it wasn't true. It was just that she and Daddy had found it easier to talk to each other because they both loved horses. But it explained why Lou had looked so pleased at the thought that he might have sent this horse for her. It would seem to be proof that he did care after all.

Amy reached the brick-walled stable block and went over to Jake, the Clydesdale.

"How are you, big guy?" she said.

"OK, thanks," a voice answered and Amy jumped. The tall, fair figure of Ben Stillman, Heartland's other stable-hand, appeared around the side of Jake.

"Got you," he grinned, seeing her surprised face.

Amy laughed and opened the stall door for him. "Very funny!"

"You know, I'm sure you think that one of the horses will answer back some day," Ben said, leaving the stall. "You talk to them just like they're human."

"So?" Amy scratched Jake's bay forehead. "They listen better than most people."

Ben shook his head at her. Before he had started working at Heartland seven months ago, he'd worked at his aunt's large Arabian stud where the horses, although treated well, were essentially part of a business. He was gradually adapting to Heartland's ways but Amy doubted whether he'd ever be as crazy about horses as she and Ty were. Well, apart from his own horse, Red. Ben was completely devoted to him.

"So how was the show?" Ben asked, locking the bolt on Jake's door.

"Great," Amy said, helping him collect the empty hay nets from the other five stalls in the row. She told him about the Six Bar and the way in which it had been won by Daniel Lawson. "But he's got a real attitude problem," she went on, telling Ben how Daniel had snapped at her after the class.

"You get all kinds of weird people at shows," Ben said. "Some of them are OK, lots of them aren't. Don't let it get to you."

Amy nodded. Ben knew what he was talking about. He regularly competed Red in Jumper classes. "Did you miss not going to the show?" she asked curiously.

Ben had been entered in the High Prelim division but had scratched from his classes after Red's confidence had suffered a knock in a schooling session a few weeks ago.

"It was the right thing to do," Ben said as they walked up

the yard together. "Red's confidence is coming back now, but it would have been wrong to throw him straight into a rated show like Meadowville. I'm going to start him off at a smaller place — there's one next week that I've entered."

They reached the hay store. "Do you want a hand with the hay nets?" Amy asked.

"It's OK," Ben answered. "You go see Sundance. He's been standing at his stall door half the morning, looking very neglected."

"Neglected!" Amy exclaimed indignantly. "I spent over an hour with him before I went to the show, hosing his leg with cold water and massaging lavender oil into his neck!"

Ben grinned. "I get the feeling that pony of yours is enjoying being ill."

Amy went on up to the twelve-stall barn. Just as Ben had said, Sundance was looking over his stall door. Seeing her, he lifted his buckskin head and whinnied loudly.

"Hi there, boy," Amy whispered as she reached him. Sundance lipped at her hands and, finding them empty, began to nuzzle at her pockets. Amy fed him the crumbly remains of some pony cubes and unbolted his door to go inside the stall. "So how's that leg, then?"

Crouching down, she unwrapped the bandage. Underneath there was a blue pouch of gel. When Amy had put it on Sundance that morning, it had come straight from the freezer and had been icy-cold, but now it was warm to the touch. Still, the tendon seemed less swollen than it had that morning.

"Time to change your dressing," Amy told Sundance, who had lowered his head and was inspecting his foreleg with his muzzle. She gathered up the bandage, foam pad and gel-pack. "I'll be back in a minute."

As she left the stall, Sundance pushed his head against the door. "Sorry," Amy sighed, knowing what he meant. "But you can't go out into the field. You've got to rest that leg."

Sundance wasn't used to being confined to his stall all day. The horses at Heartland were usually turned out in small groups for at least five hours. It made them happier if they were allowed to indulge their natural instincts to graze and socialize.

Sundance nudged at the door again, but Amy pushed back the bolt. If he went outside, he might further injure himself.

She fetched the things she needed and rebandaged his leg, wondering whether there was anything else she could do to help him recover. She was already feeding him comfrey, buckwheat and meadowsweet – all good for healing tendon injuries. She thought about the aromatherapy oils in the tack-room cupboard. Maybe black pepper oil might help as well.

She went to a stall a few doors down where Ty was grooming Dancer. He was working quietly, a preoccupied expression on his face.

"Do you think there's anything else I can do to help Sundance?" Amy asked as she leaned over the door.

Ty seemed to shake himself out of a dream. "What?" he answered, as if he hadn't heard her properly.

Amy frowned. It wasn't the first time that she had caught Ty looking preoccupied in the last few weeks. Did he have something on his mind?

"Are you OK?" she asked.

"Yes," Ty replied. He quickly changed the subject. "I reckon black pepper oil could be worth trying, and there are probably some other oils that might help as well. Why don't we go take a look at the notebooks?"

Amy nodded and they went down to the tack-room. There, they began to leaf through her mom's notebooks on natural remedies, looking for information on tendon injuries.

"Here's something," Amy said. "'Once the initial swelling has died down, heat massage with eucalyptus, black pepper and lime oils can help to stimulate the blood flow.'"

"This one says something similar," Ty said. "But it also suggests using peppermint oil."

"There's quite a lot on tendon injuries," Amy said, sifting through some loose papers.

Ty sighed. "Sometimes I wonder whether I'll ever know even half as much as your mom did."

Amy felt her chest tighten. She didn't want to talk about her mother – not when it brought back so many painful thoughts. "These notes say that magnets can help speed up the healing," she said quickly. "Maybe we should try that."

Ty let Amy change the subject without saying anything. "Why not ask Scott when he comes to see Sundance tomorrow?"

"Good idea," Amy replied.

Ty smiled. "We'll get Sundance better," he said, taking her hand. "You'll see."

A warm glow spread through Amy. That was the best thing about Ty, she thought happily as she gathered up all the notebooks. He understood her – and Heartland. He wasn't just someone she was dating, he was a best friend too.

Amy and Ty were sweeping the stone-flagged feed-room floor when Ben appeared in the doorway. "Guess what's coming down the drive?"

Throwing down her broom, Amy went to the doorway. A large white horsebox was making its way towards the farm. "It's the horse! I've got to get Lou and Grandpa!" she said, racing back to the house.

Lou was setting the table for supper.

"The horse is here!" Amy gasped. "Quick! Come on."

Grandpa and Lou followed Amy outside just as the truck pulled up in front of the house.

As Amy went over, the cab doors opened and the driver jumped out. He was holding a clipboard. "Hi. I've got a horse to deliver to ..." he consulted his notes, "Amy and Lou Fleming."

"That's me!" Amy exclaimed. "I mean us. I'm Amy Fleming." She was so excited that she could hardly get her words out straight. What was the horse going to be like? What colour? A bay like she'd imagined earlier? Or maybe a chestnut?

The driver held out his hand. "Pleased to meet you. I'm Marvin Campbell." He nodded to a woman who was getting out of the cab. "And this is my co-driver, Heather."

Heather smiled. "Shall we get him unloaded then?"

Amy nodded and was joined at the side of the horsebox by Grandpa, Lou, Ty and Ben. They stood watching as the heavy ramp swung down.

A gasp left Amy. A young dapple-grey horse was standing at the top of the ramp. A horse who was the exact image of her father's old showjumper, Pegasus!

Chapter Three

Amy stood rooted to the spot. Every nerve-ending in her body felt like it was on fire.

With a snort, the beautiful grey horse tossed his head, the muscles in his neck rippling under his satin skin.

"Easy now," Marvin said, oblivious to Amy's shock. "Down we go." Clicking his tongue he led the gelding down the ramp. As the horse's hooves clattered on to the gravel drive, he swung around, his head high, his ears pricked.

Marvin and Heather started to remove the horse's travelling wraps and Amy began to notice the differences between this horse and Pegasus. He was smaller than her father's old showjumper – just sixteen hands. His head was more dished, his nostrils more delicate, his ears more finely fluted. But in every other respect they looked very similar –

grey dapples on a snowy-white coat, a dark-grey mane, and a silvery waterfall of a tail.

And in that moment, Amy knew that the horse standing in front of her – so young, so spirited – wasn't a quiet schoolmaster for Lou to learn to ride on. She swung round. Lou was looking stunned. Grandpa and Ty looked equally amazed. Only Ben, unaware of the family tensions, seemed at ease. He looked at the gelding with frank admiration.

"That's some horse!" he said.

Amy could only nod. As she did so, the horse stretched his neck towards her, his nostrils wide. Amy held out her hand, palm-up, and he sniffed at it, his soft dark eyes looking at her curiously. Then he lifted his muzzle to her head. He snorted and then pulled at her hair with gentle lips.

"Hey!" Amy protested, finding her voice at last. She caressed his neck. "Hello, beauty."

The horse breathed out into her face and then nuzzled hopefully at her hands, just like Sundance did. Amy smiled and stroked his soft nose.

"I'll get the papers for you," Marvin said, handing the lead-rope to her. "He's called Summer Storm – goes by the stable name of Storm, I believe. There's tack and rugs with him as well," he said glancing round at Heather, who was coming down the ramp with an armful of rugs. "Where do you want all this put?"

"I'll show you," Ben said. "That OK, Amy?"

Amy nodded, hardly able to drag her eyes away from

Storm as Marvin went round to the cab to get the papers.

For a moment, none of them seemed to know what to say.

It was Grandpa who spoke first. "Well, he's not what we were expecting, is he?"

Ty's face looked troubled. "He's a show horse."

"He's beautiful, though," Amy said, her eyes shining, as Storm pushed his head against her.

"Yes, but he's not a Heartland horse," Ty said, patting Storm gently. "What are we going to do with a horse like..." He broke off as Marvin came back.

"The papers," he said, holding them out. "There's a letter in there as well, from Mr Fleming."

Lou stepped forward. "Thanks," she said, taking them. Her face was composed but Amy heard a tremor in her voice.

"Lou," Amy began, looking at her as Marvin started to carry the remainder of the stuff up the yard. "I..." She broke off. She didn't know what to say. If only she hadn't suggested that this horse might be for Lou. "I'm really..."

"Let's see what the letter says," Lou interrupted. She took the papers out of the plastic wallet. Amy could see that there were registration details and an envelope from her father. Storm pulled at the lead-rope and started to dig impatiently at the gravel with one front hoof.

"Hush," Amy said quickly.

"Here," Ty said. "You look at the papers. I'll walk him around."

Reluctantly, Amy let go of the lead-rope. She didn't want to be parted from Storm, but her curiosity was intense.

"He's seven years old, a Trakhener cross English Thoroughbred," Lou said, reading aloud as Ty walked Storm around the driveway.

Amy nodded. That made sense. The Thoroughbred in him was what made him look so like Pegasus. The Trakhener – a German breed – explained his slightly dished face, elegant arched neck and fluid movement.

"He was imported from Germany when he was two," Lou said. "He's had three homes since then." She opened the envelope and read out the letter.

" 'Dear Lou and Amy, I hope you like Storm. As soon as I saw him, I knew I had to buy him – he looks so like Pegasus and he can certainly jump. I was going to take him back to Australia with me but then I thought of you and he seemed so perfect. I couldn't help but notice that Amy's outgrowing Sundance and needs a new horse – one whose talent matches hers – and Lou…' " Lou faltered for a moment. Then she continued, her voice barely above a whisper as she read, " 'I'd like to think that one day you'll be able to compete on him, too. I'm sure that as soon as you start to ride again, you'll become just as fearless and competitive as you used to be. I'll ring you tonight and answer any questions you have. Storm's a good horse – he's won over $5,000 in prize money in Jumper classes – but I know that sort of thing doesn't matter to you – you'll love him no matter what. My two wonderful girls. I hope you like your present! Love always, Daddy.'"

There was a silence. Amy looked at Lou. Oh, how could Daddy have got it so wrong? He'd obviously meant well, but he'd completely misread the situation. Fearless of horses himself, he simply didn't seem to understand that Lou really was genuinely scared of riding now.

Jack was looking from Amy to Lou. "So what are we going to do?" he asked.

"Do?" Amy said, wondering what he meant.

"Well, we can't keep him," Grandpa said, glancing at Lou. Amy stared. "What?"

"Your father meant well, Amy," Grandpa said gently, "that's obvious, but Ty's right. Heartland isn't the place for a horse like Storm."

Amy's voice rose. "But we can't send him back!"

"We don't have the money to support a competition horse," Grandpa spoke calmly.

"Well, if we can't afford it, I won't enter him in any shows," Amy said stubbornly.

"But honey," Grandpa said, shaking his head, "that wouldn't be fair to him. You only have to look at Storm to see that he's been bred to compete, and if he's got the talent your father suggests then it shouldn't be wasted. You know how expensive it is to enter competitions – there's the nomination fee, the class fee, the travel, not to mention the boarding fees. We can't afford that sort of thing. And what about the time? You're busy enough as it is."

"I'll find time," Amy said, looking desperately at Storm. "And I won't go to big expensive shows. Grandpa, please, we can't send him back. He's Pegasus, can't you see that?"

Her grandfather's forehead furrowed. "I know he looks like Pegasus, but keeping him won't bring Pegasus back." Grandpa looked at Lou. "What do you think we should do, Lou?"

Amy's heart sank. She had a feeling she knew exactly what her sister was going to say.

But to her surprise, she saw that Lou was looking uncertain. "Let's not be too hasty, Grandpa," she said. "I mean, I'm never going to compete Storm, no matter what Daddy thinks. But it's not fair to expect Amy to give him back. She's outgrowing Sundance, and although we haven't the time or money to properly compete a horse on the A-circuit, maybe we can manage somehow — there are lots of shows within travelling distance." She glanced at Amy. "I know you think I don't always share your feelings about the horses, that I see them more as a business, but I don't think you should have to send Storm back unless you want to."

"Oh, Lou!" Amy had never loved her sister more. "Thank you!"

Lou looked at Grandpa. "Is that OK, Grandpa?"

Grandpa cleared his throat. "I guess so. He's a gift from your father and I know how much that means to you both. You don't have to send him back if you don't want to. But —"

he fixed Amy with his blue eyes — "I want you to promise that if having Storm here doesn't work out, then you'll put his happiness before your own."

"I promise!" Amy said, her eyes shining. "But he will be happy here. I know he will! I'll find time to take him to shows and, Lou, you'll ride him too, won't you?" She saw the uncertainty on Lou's face. "I mean, not straight away, but as you get confident. He'll be your horse as much as mine."

"Maybe," Lou said quietly.

Amy kissed Grandpa and her sister then ran over to see Storm. He shied at her sudden approach and she stopped immediately. "It's all right, boy," she said holding out her hand. He sniffed it and relaxed. "We're keeping him!" Amy told Ty in delight. "And I'm going to be able to take him to shows. In the letter Daddy says he's won loads of money showjumping." Excitement shone in her eyes. "Oh, Ty, isn't this great?"

Before Ty could answer, Ben, Marvin and Heather came down the yard.

"It's all sorted out," Marvin said cheerfully. "Everything's unpacked."

Heather looked round admiringly. "This is a great place. Ben's just been showing us around."

"Would you like a coffee before you go?" Grandpa offered.

"We've got to get going — we've got a long trip back," Marvin said. "But thanks for the offer." He patted Storm. "Hope the young fella settles in all right."

They got back into the horsebox and soon it was turning out of the drive. Lou and Grandpa went back into the house and Amy led Storm up the yard to the empty stable next to Jake. The hay net was already full and the straw bed deep.

"This is going to be your new home," she told him, as she unfastened his halter and let him nose round the stall. "You'll like it here. I know you will." Storm came over to her and stood happily while she scratched his neck. Amy looked at him in wonder. This was a new experience for her. The horses that came to Heartland were almost always damaged or disturbed, and it often took a long time to build up their trust. But here was Storm, newly arrived and already so affectionate. He had obviously been treated well all his life. She kissed him and went to find Ty.

He was in the feed-room with Ben. They were talking about something, but broke off as Amy came in.

"So, what do you think of Storm?" Amy said.

Ben glanced at Ty, and Amy suddenly knew that's what they'd just been discussing.

"I think he's great," Ben said. "You're so lucky, Amy. You are going to compete him, aren't you?"

"Yeah, I guess — did Ty tell you he's won over $5,000 showjumping?"

"Well, you can come to shows with me any time," Ben told her. He glanced at his watch. "I'd better go. My mom's coming over tonight and I'm supposed to be making supper. See you guys tomorrow."

"See you," Amy and Ty replied at the same time.

As Ben left the feed-room, Amy turned to Ty. "Well?"

Ty still didn't say anything.

Amy saw his hesitation and frowned. "What?"

"Nothing," Ty replied. "It's just..." He shook his head slightly. "We're so busy, Amy. When will you have the time to compete Storm?"

"I'll make time," Amy said. She could see the worry in Ty's eyes. "I'll still do just as much here with the horses," she told him. "I'll just have to get up earlier or do more in the evenings, but I will do everything."

"But how?" Ty said. "You work flat-out as it is."

"It'll be OK," Amy insisted. "I'll find the time." She took his hand, her eyes beseeching him. "Ty, please — be happy for me."

To her relief she saw him smile — a slightly worried smile, but a smile nevertheless. "OK," he said.

Feeling relieved, Amy sighed. "I wish I hadn't said anything to Lou about Storm being for her. I think she was kind of excited about the idea of having a horse to ride."

"She can still ride one of the others," Ty told her. "How about Dancer? She's healthy now, and she's real easy to ride."

Amy considered the suggestion. Dancer, a paint mare, had been found half-starved in a tiny field with her front legs hobbled together. At first, she had been nervous of being handled, but as they had nursed her back to health they had restored her trust. They'd only been riding her for a few months, but Ty was right.

"Yeah," Amy said, nodding. "I hadn't thought of Dancer."

"Lou could start on her and then move on to the others — even on to Storm, when she gets more confident," Ty said.

Amy felt much happier. "Yeah, and I'll help. It was so good of her to say Storm could stay. I want to do something for her. I'll get her to ride Dancer — that's a great idea."

That evening after supper, Tim rang. "Daddy!" Amy gasped, as she heard her father's English accent on the other end of the phone. "Storm's amazing!"

Her father laughed with pleasure. "You like him then?"

"He's perfect!" Amy replied.

"The second I saw him I thought of you. Think of him as my way of making up for all those birthday and Christmas presents you never had. Is Lou pleased?"

Amy hesitated. "Yeah, sure." Quickly, she changed the subject. "I can't wait to get on him, Daddy. He looks like he'll be amazing to ride."

Just then Lou came down from the bedroom. She had her make-up bag in her hand. "Lou," Amy said, beckoning to her. "It's Daddy."

She handed the receiver over and hung around in the background as Lou spoke to their father. As she had expected, Lou was reserved in her thanks. "It's really very generous of you. He must have cost a fortune." There was a pause. "Yes, well – I'm sure Amy will get a lot of pleasure from him." Another pause. "Yes, and me too," Lou said, but Amy could hear that her voice lacked conviction. "I'd better go," Lou said quickly. "I'm going out with Scott tonight. See you, Daddy – and thanks again."

Amy took the phone from her. "So," she said eagerly, sitting down in a chair and getting ready for a long conversation. "Tell me all about Storm. Where did you see him? What classes has he been jumping in? Who's been riding him?"

Half an hour later, Amy put down the phone. Ty had popped his head into the kitchen to say goodnight and Lou had left to see Scott. Amy stretched. Her head was buzzing with information about Storm. He had been bred in Germany, then imported by a well-known hunter-jumper barn that had shown him in hunter classes, until he had been sold to a client. Storm had then competed in the Amateur-Owner Jumper division and had won a lot. Tim had said that as soon as he had seen Storm jump he had known that he was something special. That, and the way he looked so uncannily like Pegasus, had made him decide to buy him for Amy and Lou.

Amy took a fresh gel-pouch out of the freezer and went outside to rebandage Sundance's leg for the final time that evening. As she walked up the yard, Storm came to his stall door and looked out. In the evening light, he looked more like Pegasus than ever, and Amy felt a shiver run through her.

She walked over. "Hey, boy," she said softly. "What do you think of your new home, then?" He nuzzled at her hands and she stroked his nose. "You're going to be happy here. I promise." She kissed him and went on up to Sundance's stall.

Although it was still light outside, the barn was dim and Amy turned the lights on. Several of the horses snorted in surprise but then continued to munch on their hay nets. Sundance whickered softly as she approached.

"Hi there," Amy said, caressing his ears and rubbing his forehead.

She let herself into his stall and reapplied his bandage with the fresh ice-pack. As she did so, she told him about Storm.

"You'll like him," she said and then she pulled a face. Who was she kidding? Sundance didn't like other horses – there were very few humans he would tolerate either. As Amy stroked him, she couldn't help thinking how much harder his life had been than Storm's.

She thought about the other horses in the stalls. All of them had suffered in some way and had come to Heartland to be healed. *Ty's right*, the thought came unbidden into her mind, *what place does a horse like Storm have here?*

But as quick as the thought arose, she squashed it. He was a gift from her father and she wouldn't give him up. Leaning against Sundance, she let her hands work in T-touch circles on his golden neck, her fingers pushing his skin in small circles, just as she had done with Gerry that morning. She worked her way up his neck and over his head, her fingers moving over his muzzle, gums and up to his ears. As Sundance sighed happily and his head lowered, Amy felt herself relaxing, and her mind cleared.

When Amy finally made her way back down to the house, she felt calm and refreshed.

"Horses settled?" Grandpa asked, as she kicked off her boots.

Amy nodded.

"I thought we'd just have a cold supper," Grandpa said, nodding to the kitchen counter where he had put out a baked ham, potato salad and coleslaw.

"Great," Amy said, with a sudden yawn. "Do you want me to do anything?"

"Just sit down." Grandpa started to bring the food over to the table. "It's been some day, hasn't it?"

Amy nodded. It seemed a very long time since she had watched Gerry win the jump-off that morning.

Grandpa sat down. "Amy," he said slowly. "There's something I've got to talk to you about. I'm sure you're aware that it's the anniversary of your mom's death in three weeks' time."

Looking at her plate, Amy suddenly felt sick. She put down her knife and fork. "I haven't forgotten," she said in a low voice.

"I thought maybe we could visit the cemetery to lay some

flowers at her grave — just you, me and Lou, and perhaps
Scott and Ty."

Amy bit her lip and nodded. She'd been trying so hard not
to think about the approaching anniversary, but every day
she awoke with a heavy feeling that it was one day closer, and
every day she kept thinking, *if only*…

If only she hadn't persuaded her mom to go and rescue
Spartan that night. If only there hadn't been such a storm. If
only the tree hadn't fallen…

Grandpa looked at her and seemed to sense her disquiet.

"Let's eat," he said quietly, squeezing her hand. "We can
talk about this another time."

Chapter Four

"You are just so lucky," Soraya said to Amy, as they stood by the water-fountain the next morning at school. Amy had been telling her all about Storm. Soraya held back her shoulder-length black hair at the nape of her neck and bent for a drink. "Now why can't I have a long-lost dad who buys me a showjumper?"

"Because you've got a sane regular family," Amy grinned. She knew that Soraya, with her settled family life, didn't really envy her.

"True — there's that," Soraya said, releasing her hair so that it bounced on to her shoulders. "But I wouldn't mind if they decided to buy me a horse — any horse."

Amy looked at her sympathetically. Soraya's greatest disappointment was her father's continued refusal to let her have a horse.

"You know you can ride at Heartland any time," Amy told her.

"Yeah," Soraya said. "I do." Her brown eyes twinkled suddenly. "Of course, you do realize that's the only reason I'm friends with you."

"I worked that out long ago," Amy laughed.

They grinned at each other. They'd been friends since third-grade and knew each other inside out.

Just then the bell rang. "Come on," Soraya said. "Let's get to class."

When Amy got home from school that day, she saw Storm looking over his stable door. She went over to see him, stroking his neck. "We'll go for a ride in a little while," she told him, excitement swirling through her.

Storm lifted his muzzle to her face and blew down his nostrils at her, his dark eyes trusting and affectionate.

Amy kissed him on the nose and then ran down to the house to get changed. Once she was dressed in her old jeans and T-shirt, she went to find Ty to catch up on the day's news. He was in the training ring, riding Major — a boarder who had been sent to Heartland to be cured of his bucking habit.

Seeing Amy, Ty reined the bay gelding in and rode over to the gate.

Amy called out, "He looks like he's going well."

Ty nodded. "He hasn't bucked at all today." He patted the

bay's neck and filled Amy in on what had been happening. "We've still got to work Hector, Mercury, Maddison, Jasmine and Spring — and Sundance could use a fresh ice-pack sometime soon."

"I'll go do that now," Amy said. "Then if you do Hector and Ben does Mercury, I'll ride Maddison and Spring — and Soraya can ride Jasmine when she gets here."

"What about Storm?" Ty said. "I thought you were going to ride him?"

"It can wait," Amy said, trying not to sound disappointed. She was desperate to get on Storm, but she shouldn't really ride him when there was work still to be done, especially when she'd told Ty only the day before that she wouldn't let Storm interfere with her other work.

"It's OK," Ty said, seeming to read her mind. "Ride Storm first."

"You don't mind?" Amy questioned.

Ty shook his head.

"Thanks, Ty!" Amy said in delight.

Before tacking up Storm, Amy went to Sundance's stall. The swelling had reduced considerably. Amy ran her fingers gently over the damaged tendon. Although it was warm, it was nowhere near as hot as it had been when he had first injured it.

"I'm sure it's getting better," she told Sundance, as she rewrapped his leg with a fresh ice-pack. "We'll have to see what Scott says when he visits tomorrow."

Giving Sundance a last pat, she fetched a grooming kit and headed for Storm's stall. She had just finished brushing him over when Soraya arrived. "He's gorgeous!" she exclaimed, as she came into the stall.

Amy felt a glow of pride. "I know."

"And he looks so like Pegasus," Soraya said, as the affectionate grey gelding nuzzled at her hands.

"I just hope he jumps like him too!" Amy said.

After tacking Storm up, Amy led him out to the training ring. Hearing his hooves on the yard, Ben and Ty joined Soraya at the gate.

"I'll just take it easy for today," Amy said as she mounted.

Gathering up her reins, she squeezed with her calves. Storm moved forward instantly, his mouth reaching for the bit, his hocks underneath him. With the lightest touch, he changed direction, circled, backed-up and halted. Amy felt a sense of exhilaration flooding through her. She had never ridden such a well-schooled horse. She asked him to trot and then canter.

Storm moved effortlessly forward, his paces smooth and flowing. He was so powerful, so athletic. Amy felt that with the smallest shift in position, she could make him do anything she wanted. There was a single post-and-rails in the middle of the school, almost four foot high. Amy didn't think twice. Forgetting that she'd been going to take things slowly, she turned Storm towards it. His stride lengthened and he took off. For one wonderful moment, Amy felt as if she was flying and then they landed sweetly on the other side.

"Good boy!" Amy exclaimed, patting him. She cantered him over to where Ty, Soraya and Ben were standing.

"Wow!" Soraya said, her eyes wide.

"He's some horse, Amy!" Ben exclaimed. "Do you realize how far you could go on him? USET, World Championships, even the Olympic Games!"

A grin stretched across Amy's face. "Like any of that's going to happen," she said. But inside her, a dizzy delight was pounding through her blood. Storm was more than just a good jumper – he was something truly special. As she patted his neck, a dream she'd had when she was younger came back to her – the dream that one day she'd be a famous showjumper just like her mom and dad. She knew that Ben had only been teasing but maybe, just maybe, she and Storm could make it to the top!

Get real, Amy told herself, trying to be sensible.

"Are you going to jump him again?" Ben asked.

Amy shook her head. "I'll make that do for his first day. I might just take him out on the trails for a bit. We can go out together, Soraya, if you want to ride Jasmine."

"Definitely," Soraya said. "I'll go tack her up."

"I'll give you a hand," Ben offered.

"Thanks," Soraya smiled at him. As they walked off together, Amy suddenly realized that Ty hadn't said anything about Storm's jumping.

"So what did you think, Ty?" she asked. She saw he was looking troubled. "What's the matter?"

Ty hesitated. "Storm's a talented horse, Amy."

"So?" Amy frowned at his tone. "You make it sound like it's a problem?"

"I think it is." Ty spoke quietly. He sighed. "I know you too well, Amy. You won't be happy riding a horse like Storm in local shows. You'll want to do more – shows out of state, shows in the week. How will Heartland fit into that?"

Amy stared. "We went through this yesterday. I told you, I'm not going to let competing interfere with Heartland."

"So you're going to work nights and come home at lunchtimes," Ty said. "Big deal."

"You're just trying to see problems," Amy protested. "It'll work out – you'll see."

For a moment it looked as if Ty was going to argue some more, but then he shrugged. "Whatever you say."

He walked off.

Amy watched him go. It was obvious Ty wasn't convinced. But he was wrong. She would never neglect Heartland. She just wouldn't.

"Nick Halliwell phoned while you were riding," Lou said as Amy washed her hands in the sink that evening. "He wants us to take one of his young horses."

"Oh yes," Amy said, remembering the conversation she'd

had with him at the Meadowville show. She looked across at Grandpa, sitting at the kitchen table. "He told me about it."

"I explained we're full at the moment," Lou said. She had her car keys in her hand and looked as if she was about to go out. "But Nick doesn't want to send him anywhere else. Are any of the other boarders ready to go home?"

"Maddison," Amy said. "He's loading just fine now. His owners could collect him on the weekend."

"So Nick Halliwell's horse could have his stall?"

"No problem," Amy said.

"Great," Lou said. "I'll call Nick tomorrow."

Amy headed for the stairs. "I'm going to get changed."

"Amy — before you go," Grandpa said. "We need to talk about something as a family."

Amy walked slowly back to the table. She had a feeling she knew what he was going to say and her throat felt suddenly dry.

Grandpa exchanged a look with Lou. "Lou and I were talking about going to the cemetery and having a reading," he said.

"OK ... that sounds good," Amy stammered quickly.

"OK, Amy, I'll —" But before Grandpa could finish his sentence, Amy had escaped up the stairs. Reaching her bedroom, she took a deep, trembling breath. The anniversary of her mom's death was less than three weeks away now. How was she ever going to get through it?

* * *

The sky was dark. A figure hurried through the driving rain towards the pick-up. *No!* Amy tried to scream, as she saw her mom open the driver's door, but no words came out. She couldn't speak, she couldn't move. As she sat beside her mom in the pick-up, rainwater was flowing down the road. She was shivering and wet. The trailer behind them shook as the bay horse's hooves crashed into the metal sides, but the sound was immediately drowned out by a clap of thunder. As a fork of lightning lit up the sky, Amy started to scream. And then it happened. Straight in front of them, a tree started to fall...

Amy awoke sweating and sat up. It was that dream again. She hadn't had it for ages. Pushing back her damp hair, she flung her sheets back and walked shakily to the window. Early-morning light was filtering through her curtains. She pulled them back, opened the window and breathed in great gulps of the cool air.

As her heart slowed down, she glanced at her alarm clock. Almost six. She might as well get dressed and start on the barn chores. She certainly didn't want to go back to sleep again.

It was a lovely morning. The sun's rays were already glinting on the water in the water-butt. Storm was looking over his stall door and he whickered softly to her.

Changing her mind about starting the chores, Amy took Storm's saddle and bridle to his stall and tacked him up.

He nuzzled at her back as she was doing up the girth. She smiled. "Come on," she said. "Let's hit those trails."

It was the perfect morning for a ride and as Amy trotted Storm along the sandy paths, she felt the regular rhythm of his hoof-beats soothing her. By the time they got back to Heartland, her nightmares had vanished to the back of her mind.

Amy found it hard to concentrate on her classes in school that morning. She kept thinking about Storm. She imagined soaring over brightly coloured jumps on his back, the crowds in the grandstand cheering them on.

"So where's your mind today?" Soraya said as they left the classroom at lunchtime.

"With Storm," Amy replied, with a grin. "He's perfect, Soraya." She sighed. "I just wish Ty could see it. He seems so down on the idea of me going into shows."

Soraya shrugged. "Ty's not into shows, Amy. You know that."

"Yeah, I guess," Amy said. "I just find it hard that he's being so negative about Storm. It's not like him."

"No," Soraya agreed. She looked thoughtful. "Maybe there's something else on his mind."

"Like what?" Amy asked as they reached their lockers and started to put their books away.

Soraya hesitated. "Ty was very close to your mom, wasn't he? Well, it's almost a year since ... since her accident. Perhaps he's thinking about that?"

Amy's throat felt suddenly tight. "I suppose," she managed to say. "But then why hasn't he said anything?"

Soraya looked at her. "What? Like you, you mean?"

Amy froze.

"Amy, you haven't mentioned it at all," Soraya said quietly, her brown eyes scanning Amy's face. "It's not like you to keep things inside." When Amy didn't speak, Soraya sighed and continued to put her books away. "Look, I'm just saying that if you don't want to talk about it, don't be surprised if Ty doesn't either."

Amy nodded. "I guess," she said forcing the words out.

Soraya touched her arm. "You know, I'm here if you want to talk," she said.

"Yeah, I know." Amy shut her locker door with a bang. "But I'm fine about it — just fine." She didn't want to discuss it — not even with Soraya. She fixed a smile on her face. "Come on. Let's go and have lunch. I want to tell you about all the shows I've been thinking of entering Storm for."

"There's a big improvement," Scott Trewin, the vet, said to Amy later that afternoon. He was examining Sundance's leg. "I'm pleased that the swelling's gone down so quickly."

"So what do we do now?" Amy asked.

"First, stop the cold treatment," Scott answered. "Then all he needs is lots of rest, and in a few days, you can start a little gentle exercise — not riding, just walking out in hand."

"Can he go out in the field?" Amy asked hopefully.

Scott shook his head. "I'm afraid not. If he canters around, he'll just damage the tendon again. That's the problem with injuries like this. The horse seems sound and feels better, but the tendon isn't fully repaired and can easily be injured again."

"Will heat massage with oils help — and how about magnets?" Amy said. "I was reading about them last night. This article suggested that magnetic boots can help healing."

"Heat massage is always a good idea," Scott replied. "And the magnetic boots are worth trying if you can find a source. We'll reassess his progress in two weeks." They left Sundance and walked down the yard. "So, is that your new horse?" Scott said, seeing Storm looking over his door.

"That's right," Amy said, going over.

"Any chance of seeing you ride him? Lou's been telling me that he's something special."

"Sure," Amy said eagerly.

After tacking Storm up, Amy led him up to the schooling ring and mounted. Ben had left a small course of four jumps out and, when she'd warmed Storm up, she popped him over them.

He cleared the three-foot-six fences effortlessly. Lou and Ben had joined Scott at the gate.

"Shall I raise the bars?" Ben called. "He's just stepping over them."

Amy paused. It was only the third time she'd ridden Storm but jumping him just felt so right. "OK," she said.

Ben raised the jumps to just over four feet.

Her heart beating faster, Amy signalled Storm into a

canter and then turned into the first jump. It loomed massively in front of her, but Storm soared over. A wide grin split Amy's face.

"So, what do you think?" Ben asked Scott, as Amy rode over.

"He's got huge talent," Scott said.

Ben looked at Amy. "When are you going to start taking him in shows?"

"I haven't decided yet," she replied.

"I'm going to the East Creek show this weekend – it has a schooling ring where you can enter on the day," Ben said. "Why not come with me?"

"This weekend," Amy echoed, thinking it was a bit soon.

"Why wait?" Scott shrugged. "He's jumping out of his skin. It would be a good experience for you both."

"OK," Amy said impulsively. "I will!"

Scott smiled at her. "Amy, the showjumper," he said. "Looks like it's not just your mom's skill at healing you've inherited. You've got her showjumping talent too."

Amy stared as Scott's words echoed her thoughts from the day before. Could she really run Heartland and have a showjumping career? Having Scott say it made it almost seem possible. Excitement flared inside her. If she did it, she'd be just like her mom. She patted Storm's neck. There was nothing she wanted more than that.

The days before the show passed in a blur of activity and

almost before Amy knew it, Saturday arrived. At five o'clock in the morning her alarm clock went off, and she rolled out of bed, bleary-eyed and still half-asleep.

"Maybe this show thing isn't such a good idea," she muttered to herself as she made a coffee and headed out into the cool dawn to groom Storm.

Although it was only nine o'clock when she and Ben arrived at East Creek, the first classes had already started. Ben parked the trailer in the shade of some oak trees, and then went off to check the jumping order while Amy unloaded Red and Storm. She looked around at the crowds and felt her excitement increase. She was riding at a show again – she might not be competing properly, but it was wonderful just to be there.

The schooling ring was set a little way off from the main rings. It had a course of eight jumps that could be adjusted to any height. After Amy had worked in, she paid the steward. There were three other horses waiting to jump. While Amy waited her turn, she rode Storm round, half nervous, half excited. What was Storm going to be like?

"Is the height of the fences OK?" the steward asked when it was her turn.

The fences were about three foot nine – higher than she'd intended to jump. She hesitated for a moment but then she decided to go for it. "Fine." She nodded. "Thanks."

Taking a deep breath she moved Storm into a canter and turned him into the first fence – a post-and-rails.

Storm's ears pricked, his stride lengthened and he soared into the air.

In that airborne moment, Amy's nerves vanished. As Storm landed, she felt like whooping with joy. This was where she belonged. This was what she should be doing. Her heart was singing as she looked to the next fence – a red-and-white oxer. Storm met it with perfect timing.

The eight fences flowed by beneath them. As they landed over the last one, a happy smile broke across Amy's face.

"That was a strong round," the steward said to her. "You looked like you were having a great time out there."

"I was!" Amy exclaimed, her eyes shining as she patted Storm's grey neck. Thanking the steward, she rode out of the ring.

"That was amazing!" Ben said.

"I know! Isn't he the best?" Amy said, jumping off and hugging Storm. But through her delight, she felt a faint flicker of disappointment as she realized that now she'd jumped, her moment at the show was over. She longed to be jumping Storm again. But the main classes had to be entered in advance.

One day, she said to herself, *it'll be us going in classes and we'll be winning them all!*

Chapter Five

Amy and Ben walked Storm and Red back to the trailer. Storm's day was over and Ben wanted to rest Red until his class. Leaving the two horses in the trailer, they headed off to explore the showground. In the jumper ring the Modified Jumper was now under way. The fences were set at four foot six, and any horses that went clear continued straight over the jump-off course without leaving the ring. Amy knew that many of the riders in the Open Jumpers would use this class as a warm-up.

Amy and Ben bought a hot dog and Coke from one of the stalls and sat down to watch. The class was about halfway through.

"That was four faults for Helen Pierson on Boomerang, and now we have number 45, Daniel Lawson riding Burning Amber," the loudspeaker called.

Amy clutched Ben's arm. "It's that guy! The one I told you about. He's the one who won the Six Bar at Meadowville."

Ben watched as Amber trotted into the ring. "His horse isn't much of a looker, is it?"

"You wait till you see her jump," Amy said. "I bet she'll go clear."

Just as Amy had predicted, Amber jumped all eight fences of the first round without a fault and then jumped a fast clear over the shortened jump-off course. Amy frowned. The roan mare had cleared the fences but hadn't jumped with the same willingness and desire that had made such an impression a week ago. There had been just the slightest hint of resistance – a swish of her tail as she had approached the triple, her ears going back as she had jumped the gate, a hesitation as she had met the wall. But she had jumped clear and that was the main thing. The crowd applauded as Daniel slowed her to a trot.

"You're right, they are good!" Ben said to Amy.

"Yeah," Amy said, but she spoke distractedly. She was puzzled at the change in the mare and as Daniel rode out of the ring, Amy was sure she saw a look of concern on his face.

However, the next horse was soon in the ring and Amy put Amber out of her mind.

When the class was finished, Ben stood up. "I'm going to get Red saddled up again," he said. "It's my class next."

Amy went with him. As they walked past the in-gate they saw the seven riders who had been placed come to the ring to collect their ribbons. Daniel was waiting to go in, his dark hair untidy, the reins looped over his arm. Amber was nuzzling his shoulder affectionately. He had won the class.

As Amy passed by, a glimmer of recognition crossed Daniel's face and he scowled at her. Amy glared back and marched past.

While Ben worked Red in, Amy stayed with Storm in case he fretted without his stable companion. She needn't have worried, Storm was as calm as ever. Amy brushed him over and checked her watch. Ben should be going in soon. She'd better get going.

As she reached the ring, Ben was about to go in. She wished him good luck and got a seat in the stands. The course of ten jumps was similar to the Schooling Jumper that Amy had just ridden on Storm — the fences wide and solid, but inviting. Ben trotted Red in.

Amy held her breath, particularly when Red touched the top bar of the second jump, but it didn't fall and Red cantered out with a clear round.

Ben was delighted. Leaving him to cool Red off, Amy decided to go back to the trailer to check on Storm.

As she headed for the trees, she saw a woman trying to load a palomino into a trailer. The horse was flatly refusing to step on to the ramp, his ears back. The woman was looking hot and bothered.

Amy stopped a little way off and watched. The woman tried bribing the horse with a bucket of food, trotting the horse towards the ramp, using a whip to tap his flanks, but every time the horse stopped dead.

Seeing the woman start to look around in some desperation, Amy went over. "Do you want a hand?" she asked.

"Well, if you think you might have some luck with him," the woman said, with a look of relief. "This is my first show and I sure wasn't expecting him to behave like this."

Amy went to Ben's trailer and fetched a bottle of diluted lavender oil from her grooming box. It was a great help with nervousness and Amy always took it to shows.

Returning to the palomino, she rubbed a little of the oil on her hands and, after taking his lead-rope, she began to massage it into his muzzle. It was then that she noticed Daniel Lawson. He was standing a little way off under the trees, watching her curiously.

Amy turned her back on him and focused on the horse.

Twenty minutes later, after using the oil to calm the horse down and doing T-touch circles on his head and neck, Amy at last persuaded him to load.

"Thank you so much," his owner said in delight. "I don't know how I'd have got him in without you."

"That's OK," Amy told her. "I'm just glad I could help."

Looking in through the jockey door, Amy said a quick goodbye to the palomino and then headed back to her own trailer.

"Hey!"

Amy turned round. It was Daniel Lawson, and he was coming after her. Amy stiffened. What was he going to say now? But the scowl had gone from his face. He jogged up to her, his brown eyes alight.

"How did you do that?" he asked as he stopped in front of her. "I was watching what you did. You just seemed to rub that horse's neck and face."

Amy hesitated but he looked genuinely interested. "I was doing something called T-touch," she replied. "It builds up trust with a horse. We use it a lot at my family's farm – we have a horse sanctuary called Heartland. We help damaged horses there – healing and rehoming them."

Daniel stared curiously at her. "Really?"

When Amy nodded, he shook his head. "I had you all wrong," he said. "When I saw you last week, I thought you were just a typical stuck-up show type, in it for the chatter and the gossip, but now it seems you're not like that at all."

"Of course I'm not," Amy protested. She frowned. "But why did you think I was?"

Daniel's eyes narrowed. "I saw you and your friend laughing at Amber. I mean, I know she's not the most beautiful horse, but she's wonderful and she sure can jump. It really makes me mad when people think she's a joke."

"Me and my friend laughing?" Amy said, wondering what he was talking about. She and Hannah certainly hadn't laughed at Amber.

"Yeah – that blonde girl on the flashy chestnut."

"Chestnut?" Amy said in surprise. Her eyes widened as she suddenly realized what he was talking about. "You mean Ashley? I'd hardly call her a friend!"

Daniel stared. "But you were talking."

"Arguing, more like," Amy said. She shook her head indignantly. "I'd never laugh at any horse, whatever it looked like."

Daniel looked genuinely taken aback. "Oh." He bit his lip. "I'm really sorry I was so rude after the class, then. I had you down as someone who wouldn't look at a horse who cost less than five figures."

"The friend I was with – Hannah – said that you bought Amber at a horse sale," Amy said.

Daniel nodded. "I work for a dealer in the south and he sent me to look out for a couple of pleasure horses. I saw Amber there. She was really thin and no one wanted her." He hesitated, as if wondering how much more to say.

"We got Sundance like that," Amy said. "He's my pony. He was going to go for meat because he was so bad-tempered but I persuaded Mom to buy him."

"Really?"

When Amy nodded, Daniel said. "Everyone at the sale was laughing at Amber because she was so ugly. I had to buy her. I had some money that I was saving to buy a showjumper, so I used that." He smiled at the memory. "I never thought Amber would turn out to be that kind of horse."

"Is that what you want to do?" Amy asked. "Be a showjumper?"

"It's all I've ever wanted to do," Daniel said. "But my dad..." He swallowed. "Well, he was never going to buy me a horse, so I always knew I'd have to do it on my own."

"Is the dealer you work for into jumping?" Amy asked.

Daniel shook his head. "Not really. I want to get a place as a working pupil at a showjumping barn. That's why I've started travelling up here to compete. Brad Shaffer saw me in the Six Bar last week and he agreed to put me on his list of potential working pupils."

"Brad Shaffer! Wow!" Amy said. He was the leading showjumper in Maryland. Places at barns such as his were like gold dust.

Daniel nodded. "All the people he's considering have been asked to compete at a show in Maryland next week-end," he said. "Brad says that he'll decide who to take on after that."

"You'll do well," Amy said. "Amber's amazing."

"Well, I hope so," Daniel said slowly. "But she has her moods..."

"Amy!"

Amy swung round. Ben was riding towards her. Amy's hand flew to her mouth. The jump-off! She'd forgotten all about it.

"I'm really sorry!" she gasped. "I helped someone load a

horse and then…" She broke off as she caught sight of a blue ribbon fluttering on Red's bridle. "You won!"

"Yeah — Red was great," Ben grinned, swinging his leg over the saddle and dismounting.

"I wish I'd been there to watch," Amy said. "Red must have been brilliant."

"He was," Ben said, patting his horse. "A clear round, and he was three seconds faster than everyone else."

Amy stroked the chestnut's nose. "Clever boy."

She saw Ben glance at Daniel.

"This is Daniel," Amy said quickly. "Do you remember — we saw him in the ring? Daniel, this is my friend, Ben."

Daniel nodded at Ben. "I'd better go," he said shortly. "It was good to talk to you, Amy. Are you here tomorrow?"

"I'm not sure," Amy said. She knew Ben was entered in another Intermediate class the next day, and was tempted to come back and cheer him on.

"Well, if you are, I might catch you then," Daniel said. "I'm in the Open." He gave her a quick smile and walked off.

Ben looked at Amy in astonishment. She didn't blame him — after all, just a few hours ago she'd been saying how rude Daniel was.

"We started talking," she said in explanation. "After I loaded the horse." They started to walk back to the trailer. "He was telling me about how he wants to be a showjumper and how he bought Amber at a horse sale when no one else wanted her."

Ben looked at her slyly. "I think he likes you."

"What? Daniel?" Amy stared. "No way."

"Are you sure?"

"Yes," Amy said, meaning it. She'd sensed a connection with Daniel when they'd talked about Amber and his showjumping, but that had been all. "I think he was just glad to talk to someone who wasn't going to laugh at Amber," she told Ben. "From what he was saying, it sounds like he hasn't got many friends on the circuit."

Ben nodded. "It can be lonely going to shows on your own," he said, as they reached the trailer. "It's been much better for me having you here." He looked at her teasingly. "Even if you did miss the jump-off."

"I'm sorry," Amy said.

"You can make up for it by coming back with me tomorrow," Ben said. He saw her start to shake her head.

"I've got so much to do around the yard," she said.

"My class is on first thing," he told her. "We can be back by eleven. It would be good to have your support."

Amy hesitated. They could be back at Heartland by lunchtime and she was keen to come to the show again. "OK, it's a deal," she said. "I'll come."

They got back to Heartland just after lunch. As Ty came down the yard to meet them, Ben told him about Amy's clear round and his own first place.

"That's good," Ty said. Not asking anything more, he started to help Ben lower the ramp.

"What's been happening here?" Amy asked as she untied Storm and led him out of the trailer.

"Just the usual," Ty replied. "Mrs Hampton's called to say she's coming to collect Maddison about four o'clock, so I rang Nick Halliwell to let him know that a stall's coming free. His horsebox is being serviced so he asked if we could go and collect the horse – Dylan – either tomorrow or Monday. It'll be quite a drive now he's moved to his new farm but I said that it would be fine. I've got to ring back and tell him which day suits us best. I thought tomorrow."

"No, Monday," Amy said, without thinking. "I'm going to the show with Ben again tomorrow."

"I see." Ty stiffened. "Well, I guess if you're going to a show then it'll have to be Monday."

Amy could tell she'd annoyed him and quickly tried to make things better. "Look, we can still go tomorrow. Ben and I won't be at the show for long, his class is the first one. We could go to Nick's in the afternoon."

"Forget it, Amy," Ty said, picking up the saddles. "We'll fit it in on Monday. I guess Heartland will just have to revolve around what you want to do – as usual."

"Ty, that's not fair!" Amy protested in surprise.

But Ty was already walking away.

Amy's heart sank. She hated falling out with Ty, but she wasn't going to give up going to shows just to please him.

She could compete Storm and still do just as much at Heartland, she knew she could.

She sighed. The problem was — just how could she convince Ty?

Chapter Six

"That was great!" Amy called, as Ben trotted Red out of the show-ring the following day.

Ben halted Red, a wide smile on his face. "I've never known him jump so well."

"You're a star, aren't you, boy?" Amy said, stroking the big chestnut. "And I bet you're going to win."

"It depends how fast the others go," Ben said, dismounting.

Unlike the day before, any competitor who went clear in the Intermediate immediately did the jump-off course. Having completed the jump-off course with no faults and a fast time, Red was now leading the class. But there were still ten other horses to go.

"I'll cool him down if you want to watch," Amy suggested.

"Thanks," Ben said gratefully. He gave Red a pat, and headed for the stands.

As Amy led him past the warm-up ring, she saw Daniel schooling Amber. Amy waved but Daniel was too busy concentrating and didn't see her. Amber wasn't going well. Her head was up and her back was hollow.

Amy stopped Red for a moment to watch. Daniel sat deep in the saddle and signalled Amber to canter. The roan mare swished her tail and threw her head back. Daniel pushed her again and, with an angry half-buck, Amber obeyed.

Amy frowned. What was the matter? She remembered Daniel's words from the day before. He'd said that Amber sometimes got into moods – was this what he'd meant? Amy could see why Daniel looked so worried, especially if Brad Shaffer was going to watch.

Amber's strides continued to be stilted. Daniel turned into the practice fence.

Amber jumped flat and knocked the poles flying. Daniel halted her near the centre of the ring, took a deep breath and looked up.

Amy lifted her hand in greeting.

Giving Amber her head, Daniel rode over to the fence on a loose rein. "Going well, isn't she?" he joked, but Amy could see that there was no laughter in his eyes.

"What's up?" Amy said, as Red reached forward to touch noses with Amber and the grey mare squealed and threw her head back.

"It's just one of her moods," Daniel said, frowning.

"Amber gets like this just before coming into season. She's real irritable and won't jump. The vet thinks it's a hormonal imbalance."

Amy remembered mares coming to Heartland that had similar problems. "But surely you can treat it," she said.

Daniel nodded. "The vet put her on some hormone powders which made her calmer, but you can't use them for long because it can be bad for the horse, and," he looked awkward, "well, they're expensive, and I can't really afford them. I only just manage to compete as it is, and I'm trying to save for a new trailer, so I thought I'd just do without them. It's been OK until now, I've always just withdrawn from shows when she's been like this. But if I pull out of next weekend I'll never get that place at Brad's."

"Can't you just get a treatment for this week?" Amy asked.

Daniel shook his head. "You need to give them at the right point in the mare's hormonal cycle – before she starts acting up."

Amy thought quickly. "I'm sure you can treat the problem with herbs," she said.

"But don't herbal medicines take ages to work?" Daniel said. "It won't make her better for next weekend."

He was right. Generally, natural therapies didn't have an immediate effect on a problem. "It's worth a try though," Amy told him. "Give me your phone number and I'll call you when I get back to Heartland and find out the herbs you need."

"All right," Daniel said, not looking totally convinced. "Thanks." Resignedly he patted Amber's neck. "Well, I guess I'd better withdraw from my class. There's no point in trying to compete when she's like this. Talk to you later?"

"Sure," Amy replied.

Amy led Red for a while longer and then took him back to the Jumper ring. She wondered if Red was still in the lead.

A horse came cantering out of the ring to polite applause. "That's four faults for number 63, Jennifer Rosen on Going For A Song," the loudspeaker crackled. "And that concludes the Intermediate Jumper."

"Amy!"

Amy turned. Ben was hurrying towards her.

"We placed second!" he told her.

"Well done!" Amy cried in delight.

Quickly Ben did up the girth and mounted. The prize-winners were being called into the ring. Red looked so handsome as Ben rode up to collect his red rosette. Amy clapped as loudly as she could. Having got the blue ribbon the day before, Red also received a sash and ribbon for becoming the Intermediate Champion. Ben cantered Red round the ring in a lap of honour to rousing applause. Amy was as pleased as if she had been given the award herself. Ben had worked so hard with Red and it was wonderful to see him winning now.

They drove home from the show with the ribbons

proudly attached to the inside of the windscreen. *One day, Storm will win ribbons and trophies*, Amy thought to herself.

Amy remembered her promise to Daniel, and the moment they got back to Heartland she went to the tack-room to check the books. The sooner Daniel knew what herb was needed, the sooner he could start treating Amber. In her mom's notes she read:

<u>*Mares with behavioural problems due to hormonal changes*</u>
Clinical tests suggest that the herb Agnus Castus can be effective in such cases. It appears to interact with the hormonal balance of the body, gently helping the body to self-correct. NB Agnus Castus works gradually and does not usually bring about an immediate change in a mare's behaviour.

Amy sighed. It was as Daniel had thought. But then she saw that her mom had made a note in the margin. "Can work quickly – occasionally in a few days."

Amy skimmed the rest of the notes. They suggested feeding fifteen grams daily, split between two feeds. It wasn't to be used with pregnant mares, but other than that it was considered safe. She turned the page. At the end of the section, her mom had made another note.

Not easily available in shops. Need to find own supply. Collect seeds and fruit in autumn, freeze or dry, then store.

Amy checked the store cupboard in the feed-room. Ty kept it well supplied, harvesting herbs at the appropriate times throughout the year and storing them. Amy found a half-bottle of dried Agnus Castus.

She called Daniel's mobile.

"Hi, it's Amy," she said when he answered. She told him what she had discovered. "I found some information on hormonal imbalances. It looks like Agnus Castus is the herb you want. It can work fast – so it must be worth a try."

"Really?" Daniel said, sounding brighter. "Thanks."

"The only problem is," Amy told him, "it's difficult to get hold of. We've got half a bottle here at Heartland – if you want you can collect it before you go home."

"I've already left the show," Daniel said. "I didn't see any point in hanging around. But don't worry, I'm sure I'll be able to get hold of some via the Internet."

"But then you'll have to wait for it to arrive," Amy replied. "And you need to start it as soon as possible if you're going to have any chance of it working by the weekend." An idea came to her. "Where do you live?"

"Just north of Lexington," Daniel answered.

"I know what we can do," Amy said. "Ty and I are heading your way tomorrow – we're collecting a horse from Nick Halliwell's, near Charlottesville. We could call in on the way out."

"I can't let you do that," Daniel protested. "It's miles out of your way."

"Don't argue," Amy said. "Now, where do you live?"

Sounding reluctant, Daniel gave her his address. "Look, if it becomes a problem I'll understand. I'll just call the stores in my area to see if any of them have it in stock."

"It's Memorial Day tomorrow – they'll probably be closed," Amy reminded him. "We'll see you about two o'clock."

She replaced the receiver. As she left the kitchen, she saw Ty leading Solo down the yard.

"Ty!" Excited by the thought of helping Daniel and Amber, Amy ran across the gravel towards him. "Tomorrow, when we go to collect Dylan, we need to go to Lexington as well. There's this guy – Daniel – we've got to help him. He's..."

"Slow down," Ty interrupted her, halting Solo. "Now tell me – why have we got to go to Lexington tomorrow?"

"I told you about Daniel," Amy tried to explain. "We met at Meadowville where he won the Six Bar." She explained about him needing the Agnus Castus before the next week-end. "I said we could drop some in tomorrow when we go to Nick's."

Ty stared at her incredulously. "But Lexington is at least an hour from there. You've said we'll go all that way just to give this guy a herb so he can go to a show? Amy, are you crazy?"

"You don't understand," Amy protested. "He really needs it."

Ty shook his head. "We've got better things to do than to chase around the state so you can help out your show friends, Amy." He continued to lead Solo towards his stall.

"Ty!" Amy almost shouted in exasperation. "Just listen! It's not just any show. It's important!"

Ty stopped and raised his eyebrows sceptically.

"Daniel doesn't have much money and he's really struggled to get to where he is," Amy said quickly before he could speak. "And now he's been offered the chance of a place as a working pupil at Brad Shaffer's. But he'll only get the place if he does well at this show next weekend." Her eyes pleaded with Ty to understand. "I just want to help."

She saw some of the tension leave Ty's face. "I see," he said.

"Please, Ty," Amy said, encouraged. "He's a nice guy and he deserves to do well – he rescued Amber when no one else wanted her. You'd like him."

Ty didn't look convinced, but to her relief, he nodded. "All right," he said reluctantly. "I guess we can go."

Amy's breath left her in a rush. "Oh, thank you," she said. Impulsively, she hugged him.

Ty's arms folded around her, but he didn't hold her as warmly as he normally did. And Amy was immediately aware that although he might have agreed to go to Daniel's, he hadn't forgotten their argument of the day before.

She stepped back from him. "Ty, don't be angry with me."

His face immediately closed up. "I don't know what

you're talking about," he said, and clicking his tongue, he led Solo into his stall.

For a moment, Amy wondered whether to let it go, but she couldn't. "You do know what I'm talking about," she said, following him. "You seem to think that if I go to shows I'll forget all about Heartland. But I've told you that's not going to happen. I didn't do anything less round here yesterday just because I went to a show, and I'll get all my chores done today as well. I'm finding time for everything."

Ty stopped in the middle of unsaddling Solo. "Everything, Amy?" he said, raising his eyebrows.

"What do you mean?" Amy demanded.

"What about Lou?" Ty said. "I haven't seen you finding time to help her ride again."

Amy stared at him. He was right. She'd been so busy over the last few days that she'd totally forgotten about that.

Ty saw the consternation on her face. "See what I mean?" he said quietly. And picking up Solo's saddle and bridle, he left the stall.

Slowly Amy walked over to where Storm was looking out over his half-door. He nuzzled her hair but she hardly noticed. How could she have forgotten Lou? And she'd thought she'd been coping so well — getting everything done, fitting it all in. She felt her cheeks get hot. Ty was right. If she hadn't been thinking about taking Storm to the show, she'd have been helping Lou as she'd promised.

She made up her mind. She'd been going to brush Storm over but he could wait.

"I'll groom you later, boy," she said. "Right now, there's something I've got to do."

She gave him a pat, and hurried into the house.

Lou was in the office. She looked up as Amy opened the door. "Hi. How did Ben do at the show?"

"Really well," Amy said. "He placed second and Red was made Champion." But she didn't want to talk about the show. "Lou, I was wondering. Would ... would you like to ride Dancer this afternoon?"

Lou looked startled. "Ride? This afternoon?"

"Dancer's very quiet," Amy said quickly. "I should have asked you before but I've been so busy I kind of forgot. I'm sorry."

"It's all right — I understand," Lou said. She played with the pen she was holding.

Amy nodded. "Dancer's a sweetheart," she went on, before Lou had a chance to answer. She looked carefully at her sister's anxious face. "You'd enjoy riding her."

Lou hesitated.

"Come on, Lou," Amy pleaded. "You said you wanted to start riding again — why not start now?"

A mixture of emotions crossed Lou's blue eyes — apprehension and fear, but also determination and pride. She nodded slowly. "OK — I will."

Amy was delighted. "You won't regret it."

Lou looked nervous. "I hope not," she said.

Chapter Seven

"Well, here goes." Lou gathered Dancer's reins and put her left foot in the stirrup. But just as she seemed about to mount, she stopped.

Amy saw the fear in her sister's eyes. "You'll be fine," she said reassuringly. "Dancer's really calm."

Lou still hesitated.

"You can do it, Lou," Amy said.

A look of determination crossed Lou's face. "Yes," she said positively. "I can."

Putting her right hand on the saddle again, she hopped on her foot twice and swung herself up. As she landed, she clutched nervously at the reins and dug her knees tight into Dancer's sides.

"Dancer's not going to do anything," Amy said. "You can loosen your hold."

Very slowly, Lou let out her reins. With a trembling hand, she stroked Dancer's brown and white neck.

"We won't do anything until you're ready," Amy said.

They stood there until, gradually, Lou started to relax. "I think I'm ready to walk," she said at last.

With Amy walking beside Dancer, they set off round the ring. At first Lou simply sat stiffly in the saddle, letting Amy direct Dancer, but after a few circuits, she began to use her legs and hands to guide the horse herself.

"I'll stand here now," Amy said, stopping in the middle, judging that her sister was now confident enough to ride on her own. Lou rode Dancer slowly round the ring.

"I think I might try a trot," she said, after a few minutes.

"Good idea," Amy called.

Dancer obeyed and moved forward into a trot. Lou's lower legs were a little wobbly and her hands jerked on the reins as she tried to follow Dancer's movements. But, gradually, she found her balance and the posting rhythm. *She's doing just fine*, Amy thought, feeling pleased.

Lou changed the rein. With every circuit, she looked more confident. And by the time she brought Dancer to a halt, she was actually smiling.

"Are you going to try a canter?" Amy asked.

"Not yet," Lou said. "Maybe next time."

"So, there's going to be a next time?" Amy said happily.

"Definitely," Lou answered, patting Dancer's neck. "I'd forgotten how good riding feels." She dismounted, smiling.

"I know I've only been doing basics but I've really enjoyed myself. Thanks, Amy."

Amy looked at her teasingly. "You wait — you'll be jumping soon."

Lou grinned back. "We'll see."

Lou helped Amy untack Dancer and together they went down to the tack-room where they found Ty cleaning a bridle. "Had a good time?" he asked as they came in.

"I really enjoyed myself," Lou said, glancing at Amy gratefully. "And it's all because of Amy. If she hadn't come to find me and made me ride I'd still be sitting at the computer in the office."

Amy couldn't meet Ty's eyes, she was so embarrassed. After all, he knew exactly what had prompted her to go and find Lou and make her ride this afternoon. "I'd better get on with things," she said, shoving Dancer's bridle on its peg and hurrying back on to the yard.

Amy avoided Ty for the rest of the afternoon. She was starting to feel awkward when she was around him. It wasn't just that she felt embarrassed about Lou, it was also difficult not mentioning Storm or shows in case he got upset. She was so used to being able to tell him everything that it was really hard to have things they couldn't talk about.

The next morning, Amy fetched the Agnus Castus and made her way to the trailer where Ty was waiting for her. As she walked down the yard, Amy realized that she was dreading the journey ahead. What would they talk about on such a long drive?

She got into the pick-up and shot a quick look at Ty. He put the keys into the ignition, his face unreadable. "Have you got everything?" he asked.

Amy nodded.

"Let's go then," Ty said briefly.

They drove out of Heartland in silence. Amy stared out of the window, feeling tense. It was as if an invisible barrier had gone up between them and she hated it.

Feeling miserable, she glanced at Ty. He was looking at her. For a moment, she thought he was going to speak and her heart leaped. But then he seemed to change his mind. He turned his attention back to driving and the silence continued, broken only by the monotonous rattles and groans from the engine.

Just before two o'clock, Amy and Ty arrived at North Run, the dealer's barn where Daniel worked. A weather-boarded house, a schooling ring and two barns with red walls and white roofs stood at the end of a driveway. Amy read a wooden sign by the path that led to the barns: *Jeff Clark. Quality horses bought and sold.*

A red-haired man came out of the nearest barn. "Hi," he said, smiling at them. "Can I help you?"

"We're here to see Daniel," Amy said.

The man's smile faded. "I'll get him." He turned, but Daniel was already coming out of the other barn.

"Amy!" Daniel called, jogging over. He turned to the man. "Jeff, this is a friend of mine. I'll take my lunch break now, if that's OK."

Jeff nodded brusquely. "Just remember we've got a client coming in half an hour," he said, striding back into the barn.

"My boss," Daniel said to Amy. "He's in a bad mood because I was at the show for the last two days." He looked at Ty.

"This is Ty," Amy said. "We work together at Heartland. Ty, this is Daniel."

Daniel and Ty nodded at each other. Amy saw the reservation in both their eyes, and her heart sank. She hoped they weren't going to be difficult with each other.

"So," she said speaking quickly to make up for the fact that they weren't saying anything, "Where's Amber? Which is her stall?"

"It's in the left barn, but she only ever goes into it in really bad weather," Daniel answered. "I think she may have had a bad experience in a stall before I got her. She gets really stressed out and goes off her feed if she's kept in for too long. I keep her out in the field most of the time – it's a nightmare in the winter because I obviously can't have her fully clipped, she'd just get too cold. But I'd rather have the extra work grooming than have her unhappy."

He led them round to a field at the back of the barns. Amber was grazing, swishing her tail at the flies. Her ears were back and she didn't look happy. Daniel called her name. The change in the mare was immediate. She looked up and whinnied loudly. Then, pricking her ears, she came trotting over.

Daniel climbed over the gate and went to meet her. Amber stopped in front of him and rubbed her heavy, straight-nosed head against his chest, half-closing her small eyes in enjoyment as he scratched her forehead.

"How's she been?" Amy asked Daniel.

"Same as she usually is when she's in one of her moods," he replied. "She's fine when I handle her in the field, but as soon as I try to ride her she gets irritable."

"Well, I've got the Agnus Castus," Amy said, holding up the bottle. "You need to give her fifteen grams a day."

"Thanks," Daniel said gratefully. "I hope it works."

Ty had walked to the fence and was looking at Amber. "Can I check her over?"

Daniel looked unsure. "She may try to bite – she's not very keen on strangers when she's like this. But be my guest." He led her nearer.

"Hey there, girl," Ty murmured, climbing over the gate and approaching Amber. She swung her teeth at him, but Ty stood his ground. He stroked her neck, and then his fingers began to move in T-touch circles. As his hands worked their way up Amber's neck, Amy saw the mare begin to relax.

"That's what you did, isn't it?" Daniel said as he joined her at the gate. "With that horse at the show?"

Amy nodded.

She and Daniel watched as Ty's skilful fingers moved up to the mare's head, instinctively finding the right places to work. As he worked round her temples and forehead, she sighed deeply.

Amy looked at Daniel and saw that he was looking very surprised. "She won't normally let anyone but me touch her when she's in one of her moods," he said.

"She's not happy, is she?" Ty said softly, his eyes on the marc. "As well as the Agnus Castus, I'd try giving her Impatiens – it's a Bach Flower Remedy. It should help reduce her irritability and tension."

"OK," Daniel said. "Anything's worth a try." He smiled at Ty for the first time. "Thanks."

"No problem," Ty said. He stepped back from the mare and, to Amy's relief, she saw that he too had relaxed. "Amy told me you've got a big show next weekend."

Daniel nodded and explained about the working pupil place he was trying to get. "It's hard to get taken on at a place like Brad's," he said. "But it's the only way I'm ever going to get to the top. Jeff can't give me the time off to compete as much as I need to, and I don't earn enough to keep a horse competing seriously."

"How long have you worked for Jeff?" Amy asked.

"Full-time since I was sixteen," Daniel answered. "But I began helping out when I was twelve. I wasn't into horses then but I needed the money, and Jeff wanted help with the mucking out at weekends. I started riding because I was here. Jeff didn't have anyone light enough to ride the smaller ponies so he put me up on them." He shrugged. "My riding improved as I started taking them in shows for Jeff, and then I moved on to working the horses. When I was old enough to leave school Jeff offered me a live-in job. I sleep in a caravan round the back of the house." He seemed to remember his manners. "Would you like a drink?"

"Thanks," Amy said.

She and Ty followed Daniel to his caravan.

"Not much, is it?" Daniel said, looking round at the bare green walls and old brown sofa.

He carried three glasses of lemonade out and they sat outside on the grass.

"So how did you come to get Amber?" Ty asked.

Daniel explained about the horse sale. "At first I thought I must be crazy – I'd been saving the money to buy a horse I could showjump with, and Amber couldn't have been further from what I'd imagined. But it was the best thing I ever did. She's amazing."

Amy nodded. "You should see her jump, Ty. That time I saw you at Meadowville Show," she said to Daniel. "You and Amber just seemed to have this bond between you. She was so keen – she looked like she'd jump the moon for you."

Daniel smiled. "She might not be a Thoroughbred but she's tough and brave and has a bigger heart than any other horse I've ever ridden."

"What about your parents?" Amy asked. "Do they come and watch you?"

The softness that had been in Daniel's eyes vanished. "My parents?" he said, his voice suddenly icy. "They don't even know where I live."

Amy stared. "Why?"

"My mom left when I was eight. I haven't seen her since then. I grew up with my dad in a trailer park. And he, well," Daniel looked out over the fields, "all he cares about is having a bottle in his hand."

Neither Amy nor Ty spoke. It was hard to think of anything to say.

"So, that's my life," Daniel said, in a hard voice. "And this is my home." He looked at Amy. "Now you see why I have to get that working pupil post."

She nodded. "Would you miss this place — and Jeff?"

"What is there to miss?" Daniel laughed. "Don't get any idea that Jeff's been some sort of father figure. As long as I work fourteen-hour days and don't complain, he's happy. He employs me. That's all it's ever been between us."

"Daniel!"

Hearing an angry shout, they all looked round. Jeff was walking towards them. "I told you we've got a client coming," he said. "The horses aren't even tacked up yet! Get a move on!" He glared at Daniel, Amy and Ty and then marched back down the path.

Daniel got to his feet. "I'd better go," he said. "I feel bad —

you've come all this way, but..."

"Don't worry," Amy said quickly, getting up. "We understand."

"It's been good to meet you, Daniel," Ty said. "I sure hope the Agnus works."

"Thanks," Daniel said. He looked at Amy. "Will you be at the show on Saturday?"

Amy felt awkward, aware of what Ty would say if she went to another show so soon. "No," she said. She saw Daniel's face fall. "We've got a lot going on at the moment," she tried to explain. "It's difficult."

Daniel nodded understandingly. "Well, I'll let you know how it goes. See you."

Amy and Ty went back to the pick-up. As Ty started the engine, Amy looked across at him, intending to ask him what he thought about Daniel, but the question died on her lips. Ty looked lost in thought.

"What's up?" Amy asked.

"That could have been me," Ty said quietly.

"What do you mean?" Amy said, looking at him in surprise.

Ty shook his head. "I could have ended up in a place like this." He saw the confusion on Amy's face. "Don't you see?" he said. "Daniel and I are alike. Neither of us have horsy backgrounds. We both started working with horses because we needed the money, and now we're both doing it as a career. OK, I haven't had it anywhere near as tough as Daniel – my dad might not care about what I do, but at least he doesn't drink, and although my mom's ill, she's still around. But our lives are similar, and if I hadn't met your mom, I could have been just like him, living in a caravan, working for a boss like Jeff." He shook his head. "When you first told me about Daniel I thought he was just one of the show crowd and I didn't get why we should go to so much trouble for him."

"I just felt he needed a break," Amy said.

"I understand that now," Ty nodded. "Seeing him makes me realize how much I owe your mom. She believed in me when no one else did." He shook his head. "Marion was so important in my life. I can't believe it's a year since…" His voice trailed off. He sighed. "Look, I'm sorry. I've been tense recently, Amy. The fact that it's almost a year, well, it's been on my mind."

"It's OK," Amy said. "I understand." She took a deep breath. "Grandpa wants Lou and me to go to the cemetery to commemorate Mom's anniversary. Will you come?"

"You know I will," Ty answered. He looked at her sympathetically. "How are you holding up?"

Amy shrugged and stared at her knees.

To her relief, Ty didn't push it. "It's OK," he said softly. "You don't have to talk about it if you don't want to."

Amy looked up. "Thanks, Ty."

Ty reached across the seat and squeezed her hand. As their eyes met, they smiled.

When they reached Nick's barn they were greeted by Taylor Ellis, the head groom. He showed them the horse they were to collect. Dylan was tall, a light bay of about seventeen hands. They watched Taylor riding him — the gangly bay was fine on a loose rein but as soon as Taylor asked him to collect he started to resist, and when Taylor tried to trot over some poles on the ground, he threw his head up, tripped over the first pole and then bolted to the far side of the arena in a panic.

"He does it every time. I've never seen a horse act this way before," Taylor said as he reined Dylan in.

"Has he been checked out by a vet?" Ty asked.

Taylor nodded. "Our vet says he's fine, there doesn't seem to be anything physically wrong at all."

Amy patted the bay. "Well, we'll see what we can do."

Taylor dismounted. "Come on, Dylan, let's get you ready to travel."

When the horse was bandaged up and ready to go, Taylor led him into the Heartland trailer. As they walked up the ramp together, the bay stepped on to Taylor's foot with one of his hooves.

Taylor yelled in pain, and as soon as he got his foot free, hopped on the ramp, cursing.

"You OK?" Amy asked in concern.

Taylor grimaced. "I'll live." He frowned at Dylan. "He's the clumsiest creature on this earth. He's always stepping on people and knocking them over."

Amy frowned. "Did the vet test his eyes? Maybe he can't see properly."

Taylor nodded. "His eyesight's fine. He just doesn't seem to know where he's putting his hooves!" He tied Dylan up inside and then helped haul up the ramp. "Good luck with him!" he said. "You'll need it!"

"So what do you think's the matter?" Amy asked as they drove on to the highway and headed back to Heartland.

"I don't know," Ty replied thoughtfully. "But I've never seen anything like the way he reacted when he went over those poles. It was as though he was being asked to tackle some huge obstacle."

Amy pictured Dylan going over the trotting poles. He had looked almost panicked as he cantered over them, his legs going in all directions. "It was almost as if he didn't know where he was putting his feet," she said slowly. "His hooves just seemed to go everywhere and…"

"That's it!" Ty exclaimed. "He doesn't know where he's putting his feet! I remember reading about it in your mom's book on T-touch. Apparently some horses have a poor idea of where their own feet are, so that when they're asked to do things that needs lots of coordination – things like collection or going over poles – they find it really hard and become tense and resistant. Well, that's Dylan!"

"You're right!" Amy cried as she suddenly remembered reading the same thing. "The book said that T-touch can help because it helps horses become more aware of the different parts of their body."

"Ground exercises can help too," Ty said. "I read something about how leading the horse through a maze of poles at different angles on the ground can help."

"That's right," Amy said, as they pulled up in the yard at Heartland. "You lead the horse around and over the poles and as it concentrates on looking where it's going, its balance and body awareness improves." She looked at Ty in delight. "We've got it. I'm sure this is the way to help Dylan!"

Their gazes met. In Ty's eyes, Amy saw the same enthusiasm that she herself was feeling and her heart sang with delight.

"Oh, Ty," she said impulsively. "I don't know what I'd do without you."

Ty kissed her hand, his eyes warm. "Well, you're never going to find that out, are you?"

Chapter Eight

Just as Amy got home from school the next day, Daniel phoned.

"Hi, there," Amy said. "How's Amber?"

"I don't know if it's because of that stuff you gave me," Daniel said, "but she sure seems calmer."

"Maybe it is helping," Amy said optimistically.

"I hope so," Daniel said. "It's only four days to the show. Brad phoned earlier to check I was still going."

"You did say you were, didn't you?" Amy asked.

"Yes." She heard Daniel hesitate. "Are you sure you can't come and watch? It can't be that far from you."

"It's not," Amy said. "But we're really busy at the moment. Call me and tell me how it goes, OK?"

"You bet," Daniel replied.

As Amy went outside, she thought about the show. She

wished she could go, but there was so much to do at Heartland, and she had spent most of the previous weekend at a show.

Ty was scrubbing the feed buckets by the tap.

"Daniel just phoned," Amy called. "He said that Amber seems a little better."

Ty straightened up. "That's good." He dried his hands on his jeans. "Look, I've been thinking," he said slowly. "I guess Daniel would really like you to go to this show, wouldn't he?"

Hope leaped into Amy's eyes. Where was this leading to? "I think he would," she told him.

"Well, go then," Ty said. "Ben and I can manage here for a day."

"You wouldn't mind?" Amy asked quickly.

Ty shook his head.

"Oh, Ty!" Amy threw her arms round his neck. She knew how much it meant for him to have suggested such a thing — it was his way of saying sorry. "Thank you!"

Amy flew through her work. She skipped out the stalls, groomed, made up the hay nets and then went to find Ty to start work on Dylan. They took the big bay up to the schooling ring and set out a grid of six poles on the ground to lead him over and around.

As soon as Ty tried to lead Dylan over the poles, the bay stopped and lowered his head to stare at them. Ty clicked his tongue. "Come on now."

Dylan dug his heels in and refused to move.

"Let's do some T-touch on him," Amy suggested.

Ty nodded. They worked over the horse together, making small circles over his face and down his neck until the tension started to leave Dylan's body and his head lowered. As he started to relax, they gradually worked their hands down each of his legs. To finish, Ty picked up each of Dylan's hooves and moved them in slow horizontal circles. As he lowered each hoof to the ground, Amy noticed that he was encouraging Dylan to stand for a few seconds with the toe of the hoof resting on the ground.

"What are you doing that for?" she asked curiously.

"I'm hoping it will help him focus on his feet," Ty said, as the horse moved his hoof into a more normal position flat on the ground. "He wouldn't usually stand with his toe down so, by getting him to do it, I hope I'm making him think more about where his feet are and what they're doing."

"I get it." Amy stroked Dylan's face. His eyes were half-closed. "So should we try him over the poles again?"

Ty nodded and led Dylan towards the grid for a second time.

As soon as he saw the poles, Dylan hesitated. Ty spoke to him soothingly and then, to Amy's delight, Dylan walked on. Nostrils flaring, he picked his way cautiously over the poles. He lifted his feet carefully but he didn't rush or panic.

"That's loads better!" Amy said, going round to the other side of the grid and patting Dylan as he crossed the last pole.

Ty smiled and patted Dylan too. "Good boy."

By the end of the training session, Dylan was walking far more confidently over and around the poles.

"I'm sure this approach will work," Amy said as they led Dylan over to the gate.

Ty nodded. "Me too. But it's going to take time."

"I'd better call Nick and warn him that it isn't going to be a quick fix," Amy replied.

Just then Lou came up to the ring. "How's it going?" she called.

"Fine," Amy replied.

Lou opened the gate for them. "I was thinking," she said tentatively. "Maybe I could ride Dancer again tonight? But if you're too busy then that's OK, I can ride another day…"

"I've got time," Amy interrupted her. "We can tack Dancer up as soon as we've done the feeds."

"Ben and I can do that," Ty offered. "You two go ahead and get Dancer out."

"We could go out for a trail ride," Amy said to Lou. "I could ride Storm."

"I don't know," Lou said doubtfully. "Maybe when I'm feeling more confident."

"Come on, let's go now," Amy said. "It's a perfect evening. You'll enjoy riding out on the trails, Lou. Dancer will be good. You know she will."

Lou hesitated and then nodded slowly. It was clear from the look in her eyes that she was excited by the thought.

* * *

Once Storm and Dancer had been groomed and tacked up, Amy and Lou rode out on to Teak's Hill. Initially, Lou looked worried and was tense in the saddle.

"Relax," Amy told her. "Nothing's going to happen. We'll walk as long as you want."

The sun threw dapples on to the sand track through the leafy canopy. Amy could see the tension flow from Lou. Her sister started to relax in the saddle and enjoy the surroundings.

"It's so peaceful here," she said.

Amy nodded. "I told you you'd like coming out on the trails."

"I remember doing this in England when I was younger," Lou said. She half-smiled at the memory. "I used to jump fallen tree-trunks on Nugget." She patted Dancer's neck and sighed. "I don't think I'll be doing that today." Her eyes met Amy's. "Part of me wants to just canter and gallop like I used to, and yet as soon as I think about doing it, I freeze inside and I can't."

"You'll be able to – in time."

"I hope so," Lou said quietly.

"You've just got to take things slowly," Amy finished.

"But not so slowly that I never improve," Lou whispered to herself, with a slight frown.

Suddenly the trees opened out and they found themselves riding on to the open hillside. "Oh, wow!" Lou said, as they looked out down the valley to where Heartland's buildings nestled into the mountain. "What a view!"

Amy smiled at her. "Told you it would be more fun than riding in the ring."

"You were right." Lou looked at the grassy hillside, stretching invitingly ahead. "We could have a trot," she said, a look of determination entering her eyes.

"If you're sure," Amy said.

Lou nodded and they signalled their horses to move forward. Dancer's ears pricked and she broke into a canter. Amy immediately checked Storm back so that Lou could bring Dancer back to a trot but to her surprise, Lou didn't. Holding tightly on to Dancer's mane, she leaned forward slightly and let the mare canter on.

"Lou!" Amy called. "Do you want to stop?"

Lou shook her head. Her face was pale but determined.

They cantered on for about ten strides and then Dancer fell back into a trot. Lou bounced in the saddle for a moment, regaining her balance, and slowed Dancer back to a walk.

"You cantered, Lou!" Amy said in delight, reining Storm in beside Dancer.

As Lou turned to her, Amy saw that her sister's eyes were glowing. "I did it! I actually did it!" She patted Dancer's neck. "And it felt so good!"

Amy's heart sang. She felt a new connection surge between them. They had always loved each other, but Lou's fear of riding had been like a barrier between them. Now, at last, it seemed as if that barrier was coming down.

They stayed out on the trails until the sun was sinking towards the horizon. Storm and Dancer walked calmly on loose reins, their necks warm. Amy found herself chatting to Lou in a way that she would never have done before – talking to Lou as if she were Soraya or Ty. She told her all about Daniel and Amber.

Lou looked at her curiously. "Would you like to be a professional showjumper, then? I mean, Daddy seems to think Storm's something special."

"I'd love it," Amy admitted. "But Heartland will always come first."

"That could be tough," Lou said. "Even Mom didn't do both at the same time."

Amy hadn't thought of that. "I guess she didn't." But then her natural optimism took hold. "Maybe I could."

They rode on in silence.

After a few minutes, Lou spoke again. "Say Storm starts winning, you're going to want to compete him more and more. How will you find time for that with all the other horses and your schoolwork?"

"I'd manage," Amy said confidently. "I just know I would."

On Saturday, Amy woke up to find that the good weather had broken. It was raining hard and, after taking one look out of the window at the wet yard, she decided that maybe she wouldn't ride Storm that morning after all. Besides, she wanted to get started on the chores so as not to feel guilty about leaving Ty and Ben while she went to watch Daniel.

As she went outside, she thought about the phone conversation she'd had with Daniel the night before. Amber was behaving really well. Amy pictured the roan mare the very first time she'd seen her jumping. She hoped Amber was going to perform like that again.

It was still raining when Ty dropped Amy off at the show. "See you later," he said, as she pulled on her jacket. "Wish Daniel luck from me."

"I will," Amy promised. "Thanks for the lift."

"No problem," he said, leaning across the seat and kissing her.

Amy hardly felt the drizzle as she set off across the showground.

She'd arranged to meet Daniel by the main jumping ring at nine-thirty. He was standing by the ring, watching the class.

"Hi," Amy called. "How's Amber?

"Much better," Daniel said. "She almost seems back to normal."

But Amy saw that his eyes looked worried. "You don't look very happy about it."

"It's not that – it's the ground." Daniel nodded towards the ring. "It's getting really muddy."

Amy frowned. Amber was a heavily built horse. It gave her tremendous power but it also meant that she'd find it harder to jump in mud.

"The more horses that go into the ring, the worse it's going to get," Daniel said. "There's all of the rest of this class and then mine — and I'm not jumping until halfway through."

Amy looked at the ring. Already the grass in front of the fences was cut up, the mud showing through in great brown patches. A chestnut was jumping the course. As he turned into the wall, he lost his footing and stopped, his hooves gouging out chunks of the soft turf. She glanced at Daniel and saw that he had seen it too.

"Daniel!"

They both turned. A stocky man with receding brown hair was coming towards them. He was wearing tan jodhpurs and a navy windbreaker. Amy recognized him – it was Brad Shaffer.

"Brad," Daniel said. "Hi."

Brad came over. "Hey there, Dan," he said, shaking Daniel's hand. "Looking forward to going in?"

Daniel didn't seem to know what to say.

Seeing his difficulty, Amy spoke. "It'll be quite heavy going for a horse like Amber, won't it?"

For the first time, Brad seemed to notice her.

"This is Amy," Daniel said. "My friend."

"Hi," Brad said shortly. He turned away from her and

slapped Daniel on the back. "Well, I'd better get along. Folks to see. Good luck." He winked. "I'll be watching."

Amy frowned. He hadn't bothered to answer her question about the mud. "Is it really fair to make a horse like Amber jump on ground like that?" she protested, as he walked off.

Brad stopped. "Talent is talent," he said. "If Daniel's horse is as good as he says she is, then he won't have a problem. None of the other riders seem concerned."

Amy felt the anger rising inside her at his patronizing tone of voice, but before she could say anything, Daniel spoke.

"But Brad, you've seen Amber. She's heavy — not like the others' horses. She's brilliant indoors, and if the going's good, because she's got so much power, but on ground like this, well, it could be a disaster..."

"I'm surprised at you, Daniel," Brad cut in, shaking his head. "That's hardly the right attitude. You're not telling me you can't jump in a little mud, are you?"

Daniel flushed. "Of course not."

"Good," Brad said, with a wide smile that didn't reach his eyes. "Because there's no space in my barn for quitters. You just get in that ring and show me what you can do." He walked off.

Amy swung round to Daniel. "You're not seriously telling me you want to work for him, are you?"

"He's Brad Shaffer," Daniel said.

"So?" Amy said.

Daniel set his jaw. "So, if he offers me a place, I'll work for him. He's my way out." He saw her face. "Amy," he said, "I have to get this working pupil place. This could be my one chance to make it to the big time. If I work for him I'll get to go to shows and meet potential sponsors and owners."

Amy wanted to object but she held her tongue – just. She'd already seen enough of Brad Shaffer to dislike him, but Daniel was right, chances like this didn't come up very often. "I guess," she said reluctantly.

"I suppose I'd better get Amber," Daniel sighed.

Amy watched Daniel working Amber in. Against the crowd of beautiful Thoroughbreds and Warmbloods, Amber, with her mud-splashed roan coat and heavy head, stood out.

"Looks like she should be pulling a cart," a rider on a dark-bay mare called out as he cantered past. Daniel scowled. The boy grinned and cantered on.

Oh, be good, Amber, Amy prayed, *jump well. Show these losers what you can do.*

Leaving the schooling area, Amy walked over to the main ring. The jumps were just being raised for the Open. Feeling a raindrop on her hand, she looked up. The clouds were gathering. Daniel was tenth in. If it rained any more, the ground was going to be ruined.

Feeling worried, Amy headed back to the practice ring. On the way there she saw the familiar figure of Scott Trewin. Amy stopped in surprise.

"Hi Scott. What are you doing here?" she asked.

"I'm the show's chief veterinary officer," Scott told her. "I'm standing in for a friend. He was supposed to be doing it today but his wife's had their baby early, so he asked me. And why are you here?" he asked with a smile.

Amy was just explaining about Daniel, when there was an announcement over the loudspeaker system for Scott.

"Better go," Scott called over his shoulder as he hurried away. "Catch you later."

Amy continued back to the practice ring and found Brad Shaffer with four young riders. They were all smiling at him, and Amy guessed that they were the candidates for the working pupil place. She stopped at the fence.

Daniel rode over. "So that's my competition," he murmured to her in a low voice.

The loudspeaker announced that the Open Jumping was about to start.

Brad rubbed his hands together. "Well, guys – enjoy yourselves," he said, then turned and walked into the stands.

The first competitor entered the ring.

A cold wind blew across the ring. Daniel walked Amber around to keep her muscles warm while Amy went back to the stands to watch the first few horses do their rounds. The mud in front of the fences was making it difficult for the horses to take off accurately and none of them looked as if they were enjoying themselves. Not one of them went clear.

The rider before Daniel rode out with twelve faults. The

starting gates opened and Amber cantered into the ring, her head bent against the wind.

"Come on, girl," Amy whispered. "You can do it."

The starting bell went and Daniel turned Amber into the first fence. The mare didn't hesitate. The Agnus Castus had worked perfectly and she was, once again, the spirited horse that Amy had seen at that first show. Her ears were pricked as she looked at the jump, her whole being focused on it. Quickening her pace, she flew over the first fence.

She came cantering past the stands towards the second jump. Amy could hear the heavy squelch of her hooves as they thudded down on the sodden grass. Daniel was sitting lightly on Amber's back, his weight balanced over her withers. Amy could see his lips moving as he whispered words of encouragement to his mare. They flew over the next fence and the next. Soon there was just one fence left to jump — a large oxer.

Amy was on the edge of her seat. *Please let her jump clear*, she thought.

Her prayers were answered. Amber flew cleanly over the spread and landed safely on the other side.

"Yes!" Amy cried, jumping up in delight.

Around her, the crowd burst into loud applause. Patting Amber's neck, Daniel rode out of the ring, a huge smile on his face.

Amy ran to meet him. "That was fantastic!"

Daniel slid off Amber's back and hugged her. "She was

brilliant," he gasped, his face wet from the rain. "I could tell she hated the ground but she just tried so hard. Oh, Amber! You're the best!"

Amber nuzzled his back affectionately.

"You're the only clear round so far," Amy said. "If no one else goes clear, you'll have won."

"There's a load of good horses to go in yet," Daniel said. "I'm sure I won't be the only clear."

He was right. Two other horses managed clear rounds — the boy on the dark bay, who was also a candidate for Brad's working pupil place, and an older woman on a chestnut Thoroughbred.

Amy held Amber while Daniel walked the jump-off course. When he came out of the ring, Amy could see that his face was tense.

"The ground's worse than ever," he said as he mounted. "The mud's really thick."

"You don't have to go in," Amy said, looking up as it started to rain again. "You could let the other two jump-off and just take third place."

Daniel looked torn. "But I'd lose the position at Brad's. You heard him — there's no place at his barn for quitters. I've got to go in."

Amy didn't know what to say. She knew how much he wanted to work for Brad.

"I'd better get Amber warmed up," Daniel said.

Amy headed for the ring. The rain was making the grass

slippery. The boy on the dark-bay mare was the first competitor in for the jump-off. The mare was a neat, careful jumper, and although she almost lost her footing twice, she recovered herself and jumped clear.

Amy clapped politely as the boy cantered through the finish posts but her heart was in her mouth. Daniel was going to have to really push Amber to jump a fast clear round if he was going to win.

The loudspeaker crackled. "Our first clear round in the jump-off – that was Carl Carpenter and Go For Gold."

Amy hurried to the collecting ring, the rain hitting her jacket and splashing her face. "Daniel!" she called.

Daniel looked round.

Amy climbed over the fence. "The ground's got worse."

Just then, Carl Carpenter came cantering out of the ring looking triumphant.

"And now number 165, Daniel Lawson on Burning Amber," the loudspeaker announced. The paddock steward opened the gate and nodded to Daniel.

Amy saw Carl drew his bay up alongside Amber. "You'll never get round on that horse," he said. "Not now the fences have been raised."

Amy saw a determined look fix on Daniel's face.

"Daniel…" she called out.

But Daniel was already riding into the muddy ring.

Chapter Nine

Amy ran to the ring-side. *Please let Amber jump a clear round*, she thought, as she saw Daniel lean forward and ease the roan mare into a canter. The rain was beating down steadily now.

As the starting bell went, Daniel turned Amber to the first fence. His face was white, but his eyes burned with determination. He was out there to prove just what his horse could do.

Amber sped up into the fence. As her powerful hindquarters thrust downwards, one of her hooves slipped on the mud.

Amy's stomach lurched as the mare flung herself upwards, every muscle and sinew straining to clear the fence.

She managed it ... just. The crowd gave a collective sigh

of relief. Amber headed for the second fence — a wide green-and-white oxer. She jumped it without faltering.

Not once did she hesitate as she jumped the next four fences. The trust she had in her rider was so complete and her desire to please him so obvious. The mud sucked at Amber's hooves as the rain lashed down, but she gave it her all.

Just two more jumps, Amy thought as Amber reached the final double. *Just two more jumps and she'll have jumped clear*.

But Amber was tiring. Her breathing was now audible and her sides were lathered from the effort of jumping in such heavy going. As she turned into the double, her legs skidded on the slippery grass. It was then that Amy saw a pole on the ground, lying several feet in front of the jump where it had landed in the previous round. It was one of the lower poles in the jump and no one had bothered to pick it up. Amy gasped. It would ruin Amber's take-off. She would have to pull up. But then she realized that neither Daniel or Amber had noticed the pole. They were both looking at the jump ahead.

"No!" Amy gasped as Amber suddenly registered the pole. The strawberry roan stumbled over it. It was a dreadful moment — Amy thought the mare was going to fall. But, with a desperate push from her hind legs, Amber seemed to recover. She was too close to the fence to jump it safely now. Her hooves sank into the thick mud. She'd have to stop.

But she didn't.

The crowd gasped as Amber flung herself into the air, her ears flattened with the effort.

Time seemed to slow down as Amber hit the top of the fence and somersaulted into the air. There was chaos as the poles flew through the air. Daniel fell from his saddle and then Amber crashed heavily to the ground.

For a moment, there was utter silence. The mare and her rider lay on the ground unmoving. Then everything happened at once. Stewards raced into the ring. The crowd buzzed their concern and Amy, feeling a wave of sickness wash over her, began to run towards the ring entrance.

As she reached it, the grey-bearded paddock steward tried to stop her. "I'm sorry, but you can't go in there."

But Amy wouldn't be stopped. "He's my friend!" she shouted. And rushing past the man, she ran through the rain towards the two bodies.

To her relief, Daniel was moving. He pushed himself up slowly with his hands and got unsteadily to his feet.

"Daniel!" Amy cried, relief flooding through her. "Daniel! Are you OK?"

He heard her and turned. His face was streaked with mud and he looked confused. "What ... what happened?" he said, looking at the stewards who had just reached him.

But before Amy could answer, Daniel saw Amber lying on the ground. His face turned deathly white and his eyes widened with horror.

"No!" he shouted as he ran towards his horse.

Amy chased after him.

Amber seemed to hear her owner's voice and lifted her head. With an enormous effort she thrust out her forelegs and heaved herself off the ground. But as she did so, her body trembled and she staggered back. When she was still again, she was resting the toe of one foreleg on the ground, it was bleeding badly.

Daniel wrapped his arms around Amber's neck and stroked her softly. "What have I done to you?"

Amy saw the horror in his eyes as he looked at the mare's injured leg.

"It's going to be OK. I promise," he said desperately. "You'll be fine — just fine." Amber nuzzled his shoulder, her dark eyes clouded with pain, but she looked at him trustingly, as if to say, *I believe you. Now you're here, I know I'm safe.*

Amy's gaze met Daniel's and a look of fear and understanding passed between them. Both of them knew that Amber was badly injured. Not knowing what to say, Amy touched the mare's neck, her eyes burning with tears.

"The veterinary trailer's on its way," one of the stewards called out.

"Are you all right?" another asked Daniel.

Daniel looked at him vaguely. "Me?" he asked, as if that was the last thing on his mind. "Who cares? It's Amber who matters."

"Perhaps you should get checked over," the first steward

suggested to him. "We can see your horse gets into the trailer."

Daniel looked at him as if he was crazy. "Leave her? No way."

The stewards didn't insist and soon the white veterinary trailer came trundling across the rain-soaked grass. Scott jumped out and hurried across to Amber.

"Can she walk?" he asked.

"I don't know," Daniel said. He clicked his tongue and pulled gently at the reins. Amber hobbled forward a few paces.

Scott stopped Daniel and knelt down, carefully examining Amber's leg. A grim look came into his eyes. "Let's get her out of this ring ... and fast."

A section of the boarding stalls at the showground had been set aside for veterinary emergencies. Scott drove the trailer there, carefully unloaded Amber and set about examining her properly.

Daniel murmured constantly to Amber, his hands gently stroking her head.

Amy stood silently nearby, ready to help if she was needed but keeping out of the way if she wasn't.

"So, what's wrong?" Daniel demanded as Scott finally straightened up.

"It's difficult to say for certain without an X-ray," Scott bit his lip. "But I think she might have fractured her knee-joint."

Amy forced back the tears. It was the news she'd been dreading.

"You'll be able to treat it, though, won't you?" Daniel said quickly. "Legs can mend. She won't have to be put down, will she?" There was a note of desperation in his voice. "You can do something about it — you have to!"

Amy thought she had never seen Scott look so serious. "We won't know how bad the damage is until we take the X-ray," he replied. "If it's her knee-joint then, yes, we can probably operate, but you ought to know now that she'll never be able to jump at this level again. The joint just wouldn't be able to stand the strain of jumping five- and six-foot fences."

Amy saw Daniel's jaw clench. "I don't care about that," he said. "We don't have to compete. Just as long as she's still with me — that's all that matters."

"Well," Scott hesitated, his facing looking grim. "As soon as I've given Amber some pain relief, I'll round up one of my assistants and we'll take some X-rays."

Amy and Daniel had to wait outside the stall while the X-rays were being taken. Daniel's face was set. He didn't seem angry or upset, just numb. It was as if the impact of the accident still hadn't fully sunk in. But Amy understood. He was coping. At the moment, that was all he could do.

At last, Scott called Daniel and Amy into the examining room. Pinning the black-and-white plates up against the light box, he pointed out Amber's injury – it was as he had suspected, a fractured knee-joint.

"A piece of bone has chipped off the joint with the ligament attached," Scott explained, pointing out the bones in the pictures. "It is possible to operate – the knee will need to be opened up and the bone screwed back into place. But that's just the start – it'll take many months to heal. She'll have to be confined to a stall for a time, and that's where we can get problems – some horses simply don't cope with such confinement, but it's vital if the bones are to heal properly."

Amy glanced at Daniel, remembering how he had told her that Amber hated to be in a stall.

"She'll cope," he said grimly.

Scott's face was serious. "Well, the first few days after the operation will be the worst – she'll need to be monitored very carefully in case infection sets in," Scott went on. "But as she gets older she's highly likely to develop arthritis which will limit what she can do, and she'll need painkillers."

Daniel nodded, his lips clenched tight. "I don't care how hard it's going to be. We have to try."

Scott nodded. "OK, well, we can go ahead with it, but I just wanted to be honest with you before we went any further. And we need to talk about the cost too," Scott hesitated. "It's not going to be cheap."

Amy glanced at Daniel. She'd been wondering how he'd possibly be able to pay for such a major operation.

"I've got a little money," Daniel said to Scott. He glanced

at Amy. "I was saving for a new trailer, but helping Amber is more important. Besides, it's not like I'm going to need the transport now that we won't be able to compete." For a moment, Amy caught a flicker of despair in his eyes, but then Daniel seemed to squash it down.

"Very well," Scott said. "The nearest equine veterinary centre is about fifteen minutes' drive away. It's not my practice – I'm just standing in for a friend today," he explained to Daniel. "But I suggest we arrange to have her taken there. The team have plenty of experience in fracture repair and she'll be in good hands. Now what about after the operation? Where have you travelled from?"

"Lexington," Daniel replied.

Scott frowned. "I'm afraid Amber won't be able to go home for some time. Shall I make arrangements for her to stay at the veterinary centre until she's well enough for the journey?"

Amy saw a worried look cross Daniel's face. She knew what he was thinking. Boarding at veterinary centres was expensive and she doubted that he had enough to cover the operation, let alone boarding fees for several weeks. She had an idea. "Maybe Amber could come to Heartland? We're only half an hour away." Her mind worked quickly. All the stalls were full, but they could turn out one of the ponies. It would only be for a few weeks, after all.

Daniel looked uncertain.

"It would be fine," Amy insisted, just hoping that Grandpa

and Lou would agree. She saw the doubt in Daniel's eyes. "And you wouldn't have to pay us anything – just help towards her feed."

"Heartland would be an ideal place for Amber to recuperate after the operation," Scott said. "I could take over her care, and monitor her progress."

"Well, if you're sure..." Daniel nodded gratefully to Amy. "Thanks – thanks a lot."

Scott collected up the X-rays. "Right, let's get Amber ready to travel."

The mare was going to be taken to the hospital in the veterinary trailer – it would be a smoother ride for her than Daniel's rig. Daniel stayed to help look after Amber, while Amy went to fetch the mare's travel wraps. On her way back, she suddenly stopped.

Carl Carpenter, the guy who had been so mocking about Amber, was leading his bay mare towards the barn, and with him was Brad Shaffer. They were talking and laughing.

Amy felt her blood boil. They didn't look like they'd even given Daniel a second thought.

"It'll be great to have you on board, Carl," she heard Brad say. "I think we'll make a great team."

Carl grinned.

For one wild moment, Amy wanted to run up to them, to yell at them and tell Brad that what had just happened had been partly his fault. But with the greatest of effort she fought the urge. It wouldn't do any good. Right now she was needed with Amber. She veered past them and hurried back to Daniel.

While Daniel waited for the operation to finish, Amy rang Ty from the hospital and told him everything.

"That's really bad news," he said, shocked. "How's Daniel doing?"

Amy glanced to where Daniel was sitting by the coffee machine. His head was sunk in his hands and he was staring at the floor. "Not good," she whispered. She had a feeling that the reality of what had happened was just starting to sink in. It was going to be a long, slow process for Amber's leg to heal, and there was no guarantee that she would pull through, either.

"Ty," Amy said tentatively, "I've suggested that Amber comes to Heartland to recover. It's only for a few weeks, is that OK?"

"Of course," Ty replied. "But what about Daniel – where will he stay?"

Amy realized that she hadn't thought of that. "I ... I don't know," she said. One thing was certain, Daniel wouldn't go home without Amber. "Maybe he can stay in the guest room – is Grandpa home? I'd better ask him."

Ty fetched Grandpa and Amy explained what had happened. "I was hoping Daniel could stay with us for a while, Grandpa," she said.

"Honey, your friend can stay as he long as he wants," Jack said quickly. "It's no problem."

"I guess he'll have to go back to his job sometime soon." Tears stung Amy's eyes. "But I can't imagine him leaving Amber for a while. Oh, Grandpa, it's all so unfair."

"Hush, now," Jack said quickly. "Now, look, tell me where you are and I'll come over and fetch you both."

Amy gave him directions to the hospital. It was a relief to know that he was coming. She turned off her phone and, taking a deep breath, she went back to Daniel. "My grandpa's coming over," she said to him. "I told him what happened and he said you're welcome to stay at Heartland."

For a moment Daniel didn't speak, but then he nodded. "Thank you," he said in a low voice.

"Amber's in good hands," Amy told him.

A few hours later, the news was cautiously optimistic about the operation.

"Everything went as planned," Robyn Hartman, the vet who had been in charge of the operation, told them. "Now, it's just a case of waiting."

"Can I see her?" Daniel asked, his face now clearly showing the strain of the last few hours.

"Yes, but it can only be a quick visit," Robyn replied. "She's back on her feet, but she's still very unsteady after the anaesthetic and we need to keep her as quiet as possible."

"When will she be able to travel to Heartland?" Grandpa asked. He had arrived twenty minutes earlier, and had been waiting with Daniel and Amy for news.

"Hopefully tomorrow afternoon," the vet replied. She motioned down the corridor. "If you want to come this way, I'll show you Amber's stall."

They followed her down the corridor and out of the building. Amber was in a padded stall in a large airy barn. A nurse was in the stall, monitoring Amber. "Hi, I'm Karen," she said, smiling at them. "Have you come to visit our patient?"

Amy nodded. Amber's head was hanging low, her muzzle almost touching the ground. Her eyes were half-closed and her legs looked unsteady.

"Amber," Daniel said softly.

The mare's ears flickered. She raised her head slightly and, seeing Daniel, her eyes widened and she made an attempt to nicker. He hurried over, his hands stroking and caressing her. "It's all right, girl," he murmured.

Amber sighed and rested her head heavily in his arms.

Daniel swallowed hard. Amy could see that he was biting back the tears at the pain in Amber's eyes. Grandpa squeezed her shoulder.

"I'm afraid you can't stay too long," Robyn Hartman said from the stall doorway. "Karen will call you tonight and tell you how Amber's getting on. We'll also give you a direct line number so you can ring any time you want. I'll assess her condition tomorrow morning and let you know when you can take her home."

"Thank you," Amy said, realizing that Daniel had hardly

heard a word of what the vet had said. She went over to him. "Come on," she said quietly. "We can come back tomorrow — it's time to leave Amber now."

Chapter Ten

Daniel said little on the drive back to Heartland. Amy sat beside him, wishing there was something she could say that would help. But she knew there wasn't. Amber wasn't going to jump again. The best that they could hope for was that she would recover enough to be a pleasure horse. All of Daniel's dreams were over.

When they got back to Heartland Grandpa opened the car door, but Daniel just sat in the pick-up, staring at his hands.

"Come on, Daniel," Grandpa said gently. "We're here now."

Daniel looked up blankly and slowly got out.

"I'll get some Rescue Remedy," Amy said. "It'll help you with the shock."

Grandpa showed Daniel to the guest room while Amy fetched the Bach Flower medicine.

Within five minutes of taking the drops of Rescue Remedy, the numbness started to lift slightly from Daniel's eyes. He rubbed a hand over his face.

"You look exhausted," Jack said, putting the last of Daniel's things in the corner of the room. "We'll leave you to rest. There are some towels on the bed if you want to take a shower. Just come downstairs when you feel up to it."

"Thanks," Daniel said quietly.

While Daniel rested, Amy told the family exactly what had happened at the show. "It was horrible," she said, as they all sat round the kitchen table. "It was so slippery, but Daniel had to go in – it was the only chance he had to show Brad Shaffer what he and Amber could do." She shook her head, the image of Amber falling so vivid in her mind. "I just keep seeing it over and over again." Tears choked her voice.

"It sounds awful," Lou said sadly.

"You say Daniel hasn't got any family?" Ben said.

"Not really," Amy said. "It's just him and Amber. That's what makes it all so much worse."

"We'll help him," Grandpa said, putting a comforting arm round her shoulders.

Lou nodded. "You did the right thing bringing him here. Poor guy. It sounds like he needs Heartland at the moment."

Everyone nodded in agreement and Amy had to swallow a lump in her throat.

Ty stood up. "We should get on," he said to Ben. He looked at Amy. "If you want to stay here, we can manage."

"No, I'd like to come out and help," Amy said.

As she followed them out, Ty asked, "What did Scott say about Amber?"

"That she's going to have to be confined to a stall for several months if she's going to have any chance of recovery," Amy replied. "She's not going to like that – remember Daniel told us how much she hates living indoors."

"Yeah," Ty looked thoughtful. "But if that's the only chance of her leg healing, then we'll have to try it."

Amy nodded, looking serious. "We need to think of ways to help keep her calm so that she doesn't put any stress on that leg. Massaging with lavender or chamomile oil might work, and maybe Daniel could add scullcap and valerian to her feed."

"And comfrey will help the bone heal more quickly," Ty said.

"And basket willow if she seems in pain," Amy added.

Ty nodded and they reached the stable block.

"What is there still to do?" Amy asked.

"We're behind with everything," Ty replied. He began to list the jobs that still needed doing.

Amy groaned inwardly. She'd been hoping to ride Storm, but with so much to do, she'd be lucky to get the chance. However, she'd said she could cope with going to shows and doing everything else, so now she had to prove it. "That's fine," she said, forcing a cheerful smile on to her face. "I'll go get started."

It was seven-thirty before Amy got to ride Storm. Part of her just wanted to collapse in front of the TV, but she was determined to prove that she could do everything, so she saddled Storm up and rode into the schooling ring.

Storm was as good as ever. He obeyed her lightest aid, moving smoothly through his paces, his neck was flexed, his body round and balanced. As Amy rode him into a shoulder-in down the long side of the ring, she silently thanked the stars that she was blessed with such a perfectly mannered horse. She relaxed into the saddle, enjoying the wonderful feeling of the two of them moving as one.

Suddenly she noticed a figure standing in the shadows near the gate. "Daniel?" she said. She rode over. It *was* him.

"Hi," he said, with a fleeting smile. "I felt like getting some fresh air."

"How are you feeling?" Amy asked in concern.

Daniel shrugged. "You know." He changed the subject. "That's a great-looking horse."

Storm put his head over the gate and blew softly at Daniel who rubbed his forehead in greeting.

Amy longed to say something that would let Daniel know she understood. She searched for the right words but everything she thought of sounded meaningless.

Daniel broke the silence. "I was so dumb," he said, his eyes fixed on the distant trees. "Why did I jump, Amy?" He didn't wait for an answer. "I guess I just wanted to show that Amber could do it. To prove that she was as good as any of those hot-shot horses."

"I understand," Amy said.

Daniel pushed his hands over his face. "It's all my fault that she's suffering."

"It was an accident," Amy said quickly. "The pole in front of the jump was the reason Amber fell."

Daniel didn't say anything.

"You shouldn't blame yourself, Danicl," Amy insisted.

"Yes, I should," Daniel replied sharply. "If I hadn't taken Amber into the ring, then her leg wouldn't be broken now." And with that, Daniel turned swiftly and walked back down to the house.

By the time Amy went inside after untacking Storm and rubbing him down, there was no sign of Daniel. Jack was in the kitchen, putting the food on the table.

"Where's Daniel?" Amy asked.

"He went upstairs," Grandpa said. "I offered him supper but he didn't want anything. He said he was going to bed."

"I need to talk to him," Amy said, heading for the stairs.

But Grandpa stopped her. "Leave him, honey. He's been through a lot today. Talk to him in the morning."

Reluctantly, Amy gave in.

* * *

The next day, Robyn Hartman from the equine hospital rang after breakfast and told Daniel that Amber was well enough to be collected after lunch. When Ben heard the news, he offered to drive Daniel to the showground to collect his trailer and then call in on the veterinary centre. "It would be no trouble," he said.

Daniel thanked him. "That would be great." He turned to Amy and Ty. "What would you like me to do this morning? I'd like to help out."

"Well, there's still all the mucking out to do," Amy told him.

"I'll get started on that, then," Daniel nodded.

Just then Daniel's mobile rang. He checked the number. Amy saw him take a deep breath and then he pressed the receive button. "Hi, Jeff," he said, walking a little way off.

Amy exchanged a look with Ty. So how was Daniel's boss going to react to the news about Amber?

Daniel's back was to them. Hunched over, he was talking quickly into the phone in a low voice.

"I guess we should leave him to it," Ty said.

Amy had just started mucking out Jake's stall when she saw Daniel put the phone back in his pocket and walk up the yard.

"What did Jeff say?" she asked, going to the stall door.

"He's let me go," Daniel said abruptly.

"What?" Amy stared. "He can't. You haven't done anything wrong."

"Well, in his eyes I have. You see, I told him I couldn't come back for a few weeks — not until Amber's well enough to travel. He wouldn't let me take the time as unpaid leave."

"Why not?"

"It's the busiest time of the year," Daniel explained. "People like to buy horses at the beginning of the summer. Jeff said he needed me back at the barn in the next few days. Either I go or I lose my job." He shook his head. "And I'm not leaving Amber."

"Well, I could look after her," Amy said, trying to think of a way around the problem.

"What's happened to her is my fault," Daniel said. "I'm not going to desert her now. I'll find another job. I don't care what it is, as long as it earns enough for me to look after Amber properly."

Amy tried to be optimistic. "Maybe you could get a working pupil place somewhere else," she said.

"I wrote to all the main showjumping barns ages ago," Daniel said. "There aren't any spaces available at any of them."

"Well, it doesn't have to be a showjumping barn," Amy said. "There are plenty of other good trainers around. You could train and look after Amber and one day get another horse."

"I couldn't afford a horse with the potential to be a top-class showjumper. And I'm not going to just find another horse with the potential of Amber — that sort of thing only happens once in a lifetime." Daniel shook his head, his mouth grim. "No, I'm just going to have to face it. All I wanted, all I hoped for – it's not going to happen. Not now. Not ever. I might even lose my horse..." He walked away up the yard.

"Daniel!" Amy exclaimed.

But Daniel didn't stop.

Feeling sick, Amy watched him go.

Daniel drove Amber back to Heartland that afternoon.

"Hey, girl, how are you?" Amy said softly as the mare came slowly out of the trailer.

Amber nuzzled her hands.

Daniel removed the mare's travel wraps and then led her up to the stable by Storm's. The mare moved stiffly, hobbling on her injured front leg.

Amy tried to hide her shock as she saw Amber's stumbling movements. The mare was in so much pain. Amy turned away, her eyes clouding with tears.

"I hope she settles soon," Daniel said.

"There's a few things that might help," Amy told him. "Dried chamomile or a scullcap and valerian supplement will help keep her calm. You could also try T-touch with her."

"I'd like to – if you'll show me what to do," Daniel said.

"Sure," Amy said. "You just move her skin in small circles with your fingertips. Like this."

She went up to Amber and showed Daniel how to make the small clockwise circles, each one in a different place than the last. Daniel watched intently and then had a go himself.

"You have to breathe into the circles," Amy told him. "Relax and focus totally on what you're doing."

As Daniel continued to work his fingers over Amber's neck, the mare's head gradually lowered and a long sigh left her.

"That's it," Amy said softly.

Daniel nodded and stepped back. "I'll do some more when I've put the trailer away."

Amber put her head up and, going to the stall door, she pressed against it. Then she turned and hobbled around the stall.

"Hush, girl," Daniel said. "You have to rest."

Amber's ears flickered unhappily and she went to the door again.

By feed time, Amber was no more relaxed. She stared out over her door, her muscles tense, her ears swivelling at the slightest sound.

"Try massaging her with lavender oil," Ty suggested.

Amy went to fetch it and, together, she and Daniel massaged it into Amber's neck and muzzle.

"She's fine when I'm here," Daniel said. "But as soon as I leave her, she tenses up."

Amy tried to be positive. "She'll settle soon," she told him.

But something inside her wasn't convinced.

"Scott's worried about Amber," Ty told Amy when she got home from school the next afternoon. "He doesn't like the way she won't settle and her leg's swollen up. He thinks it might be the start of an infection. He's given her some antibiotics, but we've got to keep a careful eye on it."

Amy looked towards Amber's stall. The roan mare wasn't looking out. Ty saw the direction of her glance. "Daniel's in with her," he said. "She's calmer if he's there." He shook his head. "She's got a long rest period in that stall — at least another couple of months."

"And if she keeps walking around her leg's never going to heal," Amy said, feeling concerned.

"She's not a happy horse," Ty said.

Amy sighed and went up to Amber's stall. Daniel was massaging the mare with chamomile oil. Amber's eyes were half-closed. Seeing Amy, Daniel smiled faintly. "Hi." Very slowly he took his hands away from Amber. "There, girl," he murmured. "Rest now."

He left the stall and joined Amy. Almost immediately Amber's eyes snapped open and she followed him, her chest pushing against the door.

"I've been in here for two hours now," Daniel said, looking at Amber in distress. "But it's just the same. Whenever I try and leave, she gets really stressed again."

Amy stroked the mare's neck, but Amber ignored her. She

wanted Daniel – and only he would do. She reached out and nuzzled at him with her nose.

"I don't know what to do," Daniel said, looking exhausted.

"Come and get a drink," Amy said. "Then we'll talk to Ty and see if he can think of anything else to try."

They went down to the house. As Amy made them coffee, Daniel sat down with a weary sigh. The local paper was on the table and, finding the jobs page, he scanned half-heartedly through the ads.

"Shelf-stacker, pizza delivery, telesales," he read out. "What can I do? I've got to get a job soon." His eyes flicked over the page. "Hey, here's one with horses," he said suddenly. "Groom wanted with showjumping experience, to prepare young horses at top hunter-jumper barn. It's round here. Maybe I should apply for it."

"That sounds interesting," Amy said. "Does it say the name of the barn?"

"Green Briar," Daniel read out.

"Green Briar!" Amy shook her head. "Well, in that case, I wouldn't bother. It's run by the Grants – they're a nightmare. In fact," she said remembering, "it was Ashley Grant that you saw me with at that first show. All Green Briar is about is how much a horse is worth."

"Oh," Daniel said, scanning the rest of the paper. "Well, there's nothing else here with horses." He sighed. "Shelf-stacking it is then."

"Something will come up," Amy said softly.

"I hope you're right." Daniel shut the paper. "It's hard even thinking about finding a job. All I want right now is to concentrate on Amber." He picked up his coffee and walked outside. Amy followed him.

Amber was weaving, her head and neck moving rhythmically from side to side, as she stared out over her door. It was a behaviour often seen in horses unhappy at being confined in a stall. As Daniel approached, she stopped for a moment and whickered softly to him. Daniel shook his head. "I hope I've done the right thing," he muttered.

"What do you mean?" Amy asked.

"Getting them to operate on her," he said. "What if she doesn't get better? Then she'll have gone through all this pain for nothing."

"She will get better," Amy said firmly.

"I can't bear seeing her so miserable," Daniel sighed, walking over to Amber's stall. As he walked up to her, Amber stretched out her neck towards him. The effort brought tears to Amy's eyes.

"It's all right, girl," Daniel said softly. "I'm here now." He placed a hand on Amber's neck and the mare visibly relaxed again.

Amy went up to Sundance's stall. His leg was healing well now and she had started walking him out on the yard each day so that he got some exercise.

"I just wish there was something more I could do for Amber," she told him, buckling up his halter. "She's so unhappy."

She led Sundance out of his stall and walked him down the drive. Sundance walked out, his ears pricked. "Guess you're glad to be out, aren't you, boy?" Amy said.

Sundance pulled at a patch of long grass at the side of the driveway and she stopped to let him graze. Looking back towards the stable block, Amy sighed. "I wonder what Mom would have done about Amber," she said to Sundance.

The buckskin pony snorted as he tore at the grass and Amy felt a wave of sadness as she realized that just twelve months ago, her mom would have been there to answer the question herself.

She closed her eyes and swallowed hard.

If only I hadn't seen Spartan in that abandoned barn. If only I hadn't begged Mom to fetch him that night...

Sundance pulled at the lead-rope and Amy was brought abruptly back to the present, forcing all thoughts of the accident out of her mind.

Despite the antibiotics, Amber's infection continued to spread. By the next day, her leg was more swollen and her eyes were dull and unhappy. Daniel stayed with her until late in the night. At eleven o'clock, Amy went to find him.

"How is she?" she said, looking over Amber's door.

Daniel was massaging lavender oil into Amber's muzzle. "Not good," he said quietly. "She hasn't eaten anything and I'm sure the infection's getting worse. Look." He nodded to Amber's leg.

Amber was holding it with just the tip of her hoof touching the ground. The area above and below the operating scar was very swollen.

Amy bit her lip. Daniel was right. It looked bad. "We'd better call Scott."

"Leave it till the morning," Daniel said. "He's already been out to see her twice today. I don't think there's much more he can do – it's just a case of waiting for the antibiotics to kick in."

Amy looked at his pale face. "Are you coming inside?"

"Not yet," Daniel sighed wearily. "If I leave her she'll only make her leg worse by walking round."

"I'll stay with her if you want," Amy offered. "You look beat."

"Thanks, but I'll stay here." Amber nuzzled his shoulder. "She needs me – I can't leave her now."

Knowing she'd have felt just the same if it had been Sundance, Amy didn't argue. "Well, if you change your mind, just come and get me," she said.

"I will." Daniel forced a smile. "Thanks, Amy."

When Amy awoke the next morning, it was just before six o'clock. Remembering Amber in her stall, Amy quickly dressed and rushed outside.

Daniel was still there, sitting in a corner of the stall, his back against the wall. Amber was resting her muzzle on his knees. The skin on her face looked taut and strained.

Hearing Amy, Daniel looked up and screwed up his eyes. "What time is it?" he said, sounding disorientated.

"Almost six," Amy whispered, coming into the stall.

"Look." Daniel gestured towards Amber's leg.

The mare's eyes were half-closed in pain and the scar was now oozing pus. Amy crouched down and gently touched the flesh. The skin was hot and swollen.

"It's not just the infection that's getting her down," Daniel shook his head. "She hates being inside. You've seen how distressed she is. And she's going to be shut up in a stall for months. How can I put her through this, Amy?"

"Because you love her," Amy said firmly. "Because there's nothing else you can do. Let's get hold of Scott — he'll give her some more painkillers," Amy said desperately. "She'll feel better then."

When Scott arrived an hour later, Amy could see from the look in his eyes the truth of the situation.

"I can give her another shot of antibiotics and we'll see how she goes, but it's not looking too promising," he said, softly patting Amber's neck as he came out of her stall. "I'll come back first thing tomorrow and see how she is then, but if she's no better, we might have to think of alternatives."

"Alternatives?" Daniel's eyes flashed angrily. "What do you mean, alternatives?"

Scott shrugged, looking embarrassed. "You have to think

of what's best for the horse." Scott tried to put a hand on Daniel's shoulder, but he shrugged it off.

"I'm not giving up on her," Daniel said. "She'll pull through this. I'm not having her put down. Look, she's still fighting." Daniel lifted his hand towards his horse and she seemed to look back at him with as much willpower as she could muster.

"Maybe," Scott shrugged, but Amy could hear the hesitation in his words. He was trying to be kind to Daniel, but he clearly didn't want to give them false hope.

Amy woke even earlier the next day. For one small moment, she thought that everything was all right. But then she remembered – Amber. Scott was coming over early to assess her progress this morning. Quickly she got out of bed, dressed and ran down the stairs. The first rays of light were slowly sweeping across the yard as she ran into the barn and down to Amber's stall. There, as she expected, she found Daniel in the stall, beside the mare. His clothes were ruffled and his face tear-stained. At Amy's approach, Daniel looked up.

"How is she?" Amy asked gently.

"She's worse ... *much* worse," Daniel swallowed. "The swelling in her leg ... it feels on fire, and she barely seems to recognize me."

Amy didn't know what to say. Scott's words from yesterday rang in her ears as she reached forward to stroke Amber's neck. The mare didn't move a muscle. Her eyes, always so reflective, were now dull and listless. It was as though a light had gone out in them.

"I'll go and get her morning feed," Amy said hurriedly. Quickly, she turned and made her way to the feed-room. As Amy scooped the food into a bucket, she felt a lump rising in her throat.

When Amy returned with the feed, Daniel was already on his feet.

"Here you are, Amber," he crooned, offering her the mixture.

But Amber didn't even look at him. She just stood there, her eyes half-closed.

Daniel blinked and Amy saw that his eyes were glinting with tears.

"She's not even interested in food," he said. "I've been sitting here thinking, Amy – thinking about what Scott was saying yesterday. And you know, if you love someone you don't let them suffer. You do what's best for them."

Amy felt cold. She heard footsteps behind her and was relieved to see Ty's comforting face. She knew what Daniel was about to say, knew what he was thinking, but it was too awful ... and a decision that only Daniel could make.

Just at that moment, she heard the slamming of a car door, then feet on gravel. Scott appeared in the doorway.

Slowly the vet walked forward and gently worked his hands down Amber's legs. Amber didn't move a muscle. Scott didn't need to say anything, his face said enough.

"It's bad, Daniel—"

But before Scott could go on, Daniel stopped him mid-flow. "I've come to a decision," he said slowly. "I was stupid to think that a day would make any difference – I know she's in a lot of pain. It would be kinder to … to…"

"We could persevere with fighting the infection," Scott stepped in. "But even if she does get through the infection period, we would still have months of recovery time ahead of us, months of pain when she might not be any better by the end of it."

"I know."

Standing in the doorway, Amy felt her heart breaking for Daniel. She knew what it was like to have to make such a decision. She'd had to do it herself with Pegasus.

Daniel touched Amber's face. "This isn't fair on you, girl," he whispered. "I can't let you suffer." He glanced round at Scott. "Will … will you put her to sleep, please?" On the last word, his voice cracked.

Hot tears pricked the back of Amy's eyes and she swallowed hard.

Scott nodded. "If it's any help I think it's the right decision to make," he said gently. "You've done everything you can to help her, Daniel. No one could have done more. And if this is going to be the way things end – better to do it sooner than to keep her in pain." He touched Daniel's arm in sympathy. "I'll go get my bag."

As Scott prepared the injection, Daniel slowly stroked

Amber's face, tears coursing down his face. Then as Scott administered the drug, he held Amber's halter and kissed her goodbye.

At first nothing happened, but then Amber's legs wobbled. She staggered and slowly sank to the floor.

Crouching down beside her, Daniel cradled her head in his arms. "Please forgive me," he whispered in desperation. "Please forgive me," he repeated, hoping that she might hear his voice one more time.

The mare's eyelids flickered. For a long moment, she stared up at him with a look brimming with love and trust. Then a deep sigh left her and she was still.

Scott put his hand on Daniel's shoulder and spoke softly, "She's gone, Daniel. She's gone."

Chapter Eleven

It was over. Amy turned her face into Ty's chest. He held her tightly, strong and comforting, as she fought hard to get herself under control. She had to be strong, for Daniel's sake. He was the one who needed the support now. Choking back the tears, she pulled away from Ty and moved over to Daniel, crouched beside Amber.

"Daniel," she whispered, her voice shaking.

He stood up and, without saying a word, pushed past her and ran into the house.

To Amy's relief, Grandpa agreed that she could stay home from school that day. After lunch, she went to try and talk to Daniel, but he wouldn't come out of his room.

"Please," he said through the door. "I just need to be on my own."

Amy understood. After her mom had died, all she had

wanted to do was shut out the world. So she left him to grieve. Going up to Storm's stall, she put her arms round the gelding's strong, warm neck.

"Why do these things have to happen?" she whispered, resting her cheek against his warm skin.

But she knew only too well that there was never an answer to that.

That day and night, Daniel stayed in his room. But the following morning, when Amy came back from riding Storm on the trails, she saw him on the yard, pushing a wheelbarrow.

"Daniel!" she said, riding Storm over. "How are you?"

"Busy." His eyes were bleak. "I've been cleaning out Amber's stall."

Amy stared. "You didn't have to do that."

"I have to," Daniel said setting his shoulders and continuing up the yard.

Later, Amy spoke to Grandpa about him.

"There's little we can do at the moment," he said. "Except be here for him. I've told Daniel he can stay as long as he wants to." He looked at her in concern. "You look tired."

"I am," Amy admitted. "There's just so much to do at the moment — all the horses and school stuff, and now Daniel."

"And you've been getting up very early to ride Storm," Grandpa commented, starting to wash up the breakfast dishes.

"I don't mind that," Amy replied.

"Maybe Lou could help," Grandpa said thoughtfully. "She's been saying how much she likes riding again. Couldn't she ride Storm sometimes?"

Amy considered it. "I think he'd be too much for her," she said slowly. "He's really well schooled but he is spirited and if he played up, Lou might lose her confidence all over again."

"That wouldn't be good," Grandpa said. "Well, maybe in time."

"Yeah, maybe," Amy agreed.

Grandpa frowned. "But that doesn't help with the fact that there aren't enough hours in the day for you right now."

Amy stifled a yawn. "I'm fine," she reassured him as brightly as she could. "Don't worry about me, Grandpa. I can cope."

However, despite her words, Amy had to stop herself from falling asleep several times in class that day. She felt exhausted, and it wasn't just because of all the work at Heartland. Every night she was plagued with nightmares about her mom's accident. It would be a year tomorrow that it had happened, and although Amy was trying not to think about it, it was as if there was a clock ticking away hours in her head.

It didn't help when, in creative writing class that day, Mrs Schwartz, their teacher, asked them to write a piece about the person who had been most important in their life.

"So who did you write about?" Soraya asked as they packed up their stuff after class. "Was it your——?"

"Grandpa," Amy interrupted her. "I wrote about Grandpa."

"Oh, right." Soraya looked at her quizzically but to Amy's relief didn't say anything. Amy picked up her books. She knew Soraya was still worried that she wasn't talking about the anniversary of her mom's death, but she just couldn't. It was far better to try and put it, and the bad dreams, right out of her mind.

"Hey, what's the rush?" Ty said, as he came across Amy sweeping the floor of the hay store later that afternoon. "Slow down or you'll brush the floor away."

"I'm just trying to get things done," Amy said.

To her relief, Ty didn't question her any further. With a shrug, he went to the feed-room.

Amy put the broom away and was heading back to help him when she saw Daniel coming out of the tack-room. It was the first time they'd met since that morning. He looked desolate.

"Hi," Amy said. "Ty and I could use a hand with the feeds. Have you got time to help?"

At first Amy thought Daniel was going to make an excuse, but then he nodded and followed her up to the feed-room. Ty exchanged looks with Amy. She shrugged. She didn't know why she'd asked Daniel to help, she just felt that it would do him good to start doing things again. As they began to measure out and mix the feeds, she tried to think of something to say, but Daniel broke the silence.

"I've decided to apply for that job in the paper," he said. "At that local hunter barn."

"Do you mean Green Briar?" Ty asked.

"But don't you remember what I told you about the Grants – they're just out to make money," Amy said in astonishment.

Daniel shrugged. "That's OK by me. A job where the horses are just business will suit me fine."

"You don't mean that," Amy said.

"Yes, I do," Daniel said bleakly. "Something with no emotional involvement is just what I need. I'm applying." He looked at them almost defiantly. "Whatever you say." He started to mix the feeds.

Amy opened her mouth to protest, but before the words could leave her mouth, Ty had started to speak. "Well, you have to do what you think is best," he said to Daniel. "Whatever you decide, we'll back you up."

Amy stared at him. Catching her look, Ty nodded meaningfully in Daniel's direction. Amy's eyes followed his gaze. Daniel was bent over the feed buckets, his face utterly forlorn. And suddenly Amy knew that, much as it would cost her, Daniel needed their support. "If you want to work at Green Briar, that's fine by us," she managed to say, the words cutting through her like knives.

Daniel looked up in surprise. "You mean it?"

They both nodded.

A trace of a smile flickered across Daniel's face. "Thanks," he said, turning back to the feeds. "I appreciate that."

Amy had just come in from the yard for the evening when Nick Halliwell rang to check on Dylan's progress.

"He's doing well," Amy told him. "His coordination and balance seem to be improving, and he seems happier. We thought we'd try riding him in the next few days."

"Good news," Nick said. "I'll stop by on the weekend and see him."

"Sure." Then Amy remembered, and she had to swallow back the nausea that churned in her stomach. "Sorry — Saturday isn't such a good day," she said.

To her relief, Nick didn't ask why. "Fine," he said easily. "Sunday then."

Amy was about to say goodbye when an idea suddenly struck her. A brilliant idea. Why hadn't she thought about it before? "Nick," she said quickly. "You haven't got any working pupil places coming up, have you?"

"Working pupil places?" Nick said, sounding surprised. "I haven't, I'm afraid. Why?"

"It's for a friend," Amy explained. "You've met him. He's called Daniel Lawson. He won the Six Bar at the Meadowville Show. Do you remember?"

"I remember," Nick said. "He was good. But I filled a position just six weeks ago."

"Oh," Amy said.

Nick sounded genuinely sorry. "If anything comes up, I'll let you know."

"Thanks, Nick," Amy said, and she put down the phone. As she turned, she jumped. Daniel was standing in the kitchen doorway. "Daniel!" Amy said, wondering how long he'd been there.

Daniel was frowning. "Who was that on the phone? You were talking about me."

"It was Nick Halliwell," Amy explained. "The showjumper – he owns Dylan. I just thought I'd ask him if he had any working pupil places that you could have. But he hasn't."

"I told you at feed time – I'm going to apply for that job at Green Briar," Daniel said abruptly.

"Yeah, I know," Amy said. "It's just … well, there's no need to rush into anything, is there? Grandpa's said you can stay here as long as you want. Why don't you wait for a bit – maybe a working pupil place will come up at another jumper barn?"

For a moment she thought Daniel looked torn, but then his jaw tightened. "I don't want to wait." He shook his head. "I told you, I'm not going to be a showjumper any more."

Amy stared. "But you don't really mean that."

"Don't I?" Daniel walked to the table, his face bleak. "I had my chance, Amy, and I blew it. I've got to accept that and move on. My dreams are over."

"But that's dumb," Amy protested.

Daniel looked at her angrily. "No, it's not!" He swung round and marched out of the room.

Amy ran after him. "Daniel!" She grabbed his arm as he reached the top of the stairs.

Daniel took a deep breath. "I've got to be realistic, Amy," he said, his voice tight. "I can't wait round for the perfect job. I need to get on with my life."

But not in this way. Amy could feel the words burning on her lips but she bit them back.

"I rang Green Briar after we fed the horses," Daniel went on. "They've invited me round for an interview first thing tomorrow." His eyes met hers. "If they offer me a job I'm going to take it."

Amy swallowed. "I see."

Turning abruptly, Daniel continued to his room.

Amy watched him go and, as his door shut, she sighed wearily and headed back downstairs. Lou was coming out of the living room.

"The flowers for tomorrow arrived earlier," Lou said. "They're through here if you want to see them."

Amy's stomach lurched. "No, no, it's all right," she stammered.

"Are you sure?" Lou asked.

"Yes," Amy said, and, feeling sick, she hurried past Lou and into the kitchen.

Chapter Twelve

The rain was beating down, bouncing in the puddles. The sky was dark. A woman was standing by the pick-up truck, her blonde hair plastered to her head by the rain, her face sad.

"Mom," Amy whispered, running towards her.

"You asked me to go, Amy," her mom said, shaking her head.

Tears of despair ran down Amy's cheeks, mixing with the rain. "Oh, Mom," she sobbed. "I'm so sorry!"

Amy sat upright in her bed; the grey dawn light was filtering through the curtains. She pushed her hands over her face and took a deep breath. The day had finally come — the day she'd been dreading.

She got up, pulled on her clothes and went outside.

The morning was cool and fresh, the sun just rising in the sky.

Amy walked slowly up to Sundance's stall. He lifted his head and whickered in surprise when he saw her. She rubbed his golden face and leaned her head against his. He nuzzled her curiously.

I want to forget, Amy thought. *I just want to forget.*

After putting his halter on, Amy led him outside. His hooves clattered loudly on the concrete, the sound carrying in the silent morning air. Some of the other horses looked hopefully out over their doors as if they thought it might be breakfast time. But as Amy led Sundance over to graze on the grass at the side of the driveway, they lost interest and went back inside their stalls.

A year ago today...

As Sundance started to pull at the long grass, Amy sank down on her knees. Shutting her eyes, she began to relive the day exactly a year before. She saw it all again – Spartan abandoned in the barn, the gallop home through the rain, her and her mom setting out in the trailer...

"Amy?"

Amy's eyes sprang open. Daniel was standing in front of her, his face frowning in concern. "Are you OK? I saw you from my bedroom window. What are you doing?"

Amy couldn't answer. Tears choked her. As her eyes filled up, Daniel's frown quickly deepened. "What's the matter?" he asked.

"Nothing," Amy tried to say, but a sob burst from her. "Everything," she sobbed incoherently, burying her head in her knees. "Just everything."

She felt Daniel's hand on her shoulder. "Amy — what is it?" he said, crouching beside her.

He sounded so worried, Amy made herself explain. "It's my mom — she died a year ago today."

"I … I'm so sorry," Daniel said. He shook his head. "Sometimes words can be inadequate."

"It's OK," Amy muttered, brushing her tears away with the back of her hand and standing up.

"How did she die?" Daniel asked quietly.

"It was a road accident," Amy stroked Sundance and forced the words past the painful lump in her throat. "We were rescuing a horse. There was a storm, and a tree fell on the trailer." Fresh tears sprang to her eyes. "I persuaded her to go out, even though the weather was bad." Her voice choked. "It was all my fault."

"I'm sure it wasn't," Daniel said.

"It was," Amy whispered.

There was a pause. "Sometimes accidents just happen," Daniel said at last. "Deep down we both know that. You want to be angry with yourself because it's easier to cope if you take the blame." He shook his head. "But blaming yourself for something that wasn't your fault doesn't help anyone, and it was you who made me realize that."

Amy looked up in surprise. "Me?" she stammered.

Daniel nodded. "What you said yesterday — it was right, even if I didn't want to hear it. I *have* been trying to punish myself for what happened to Amber, but the accident wasn't my fault." He looked at his hands for a moment. "It just seemed easier to cope with her death if I had someone to be angry at — even if it was myself." He glanced at her. "Does that make me sound crazy?"

"No," Amy answered slowly. She knew what he was getting at. In fact, she was beginning to think that it was exactly what she had been doing over the last year.

"I think it's like, deep down, we want to believe that everything that happens, happens for a reason," Daniel went on. "But it doesn't. Life isn't like that. Sometimes people are just in the wrong place at the wrong time."

Amy nodded sadly, as Sundance pushed at her hands with his muzzle. She knew he was right.

Daniel rubbed her shoulder. "I figure you need to take the advice you gave me — accept that what happened to your mom was an accident, let go of the guilt and move on."

Amy couldn't speak. Daniel put an arm around her and she leaned against him.

"Do you think the pain ever goes away?" she asked in trembling voice.

"No," Daniel replied softly. "But I think it gets easier. You'll never forget your mom and I'll never forget Amber. They'll always be there in our hearts, but we have to live our lives. We've got to take what they've given us and move on."

For a moment they were both silent in their memories.

At last, Amy sighed. "Thanks," she said, looking up at Daniel.

"It's OK." Daniel smiled. "Thank you for making me realize that I can't stay stuck in the past for ever."

"So are you really going to go for this interview at Green Briar?" Amy asked him.

"Yes," Daniel replied. "It might not be the ideal barn, but right now I just need some time to get myself sorted out, no emotional involvement, just time to decide what I want to do."

"Does that mean that you might still try and get a working pupil place at a jumper barn one day?" Amy asked hopefully.

"Maybe," Daniel replied.

"So, you haven't given up your dream for ever," Amy said quickly.

Daniel shrugged. "Not for ever," he said slowly. "But right now, I'm going to take things one step at a time."

Amy smiled. "Me too," she said.

She patted Sundance. *Yes*, she thought firmly. *Me too*.

When Ty and Ben arrived, Amy and Daniel were chatting and giving out the morning feeds.

Amy saw Ty's surprised look.

"Daniel looks happier," he said when they were alone.

"Yeah," Amy said, nodding. "I think he is."

At nine o'clock, Daniel left to go to Green Briar. He

returned an hour later with the news that he had accepted the job.

"Val Grant was keen to take me on when they heard about all my jumping experience," he told Amy, as she met him by his pick-up. "I think she's planning to develop the jumping side of Green Briar's business. She offered me the job on the spot."

Amy couldn't get too exited by the prospect but she forced a smile. "Congratulations." She tried to look on the bright side. "At least you'll still be living close by. You can come and visit whenever you want."

"Just try and keep me away," Daniel said. He raised his eyebrows. "And, who knows, maybe I'll even be able to convert Val Grant to Heartland's methods one day."

Amy laughed. "Yeah, right!"

Daniel smiled at her. "Look, thanks for everything, Amy — you've been a really good friend."

"I'm just sorry I shouted at you last night," Amy sighed. "I wasn't exactly sensitive."

Daniel grinned. "Well, I needed someone to say those things. And anyway, judging by the way Storm's been jumping, I'll be seeing you at shows most weekends. It's not going to be long before you and Storm are winning your way round the A-circuit."

"In my dreams!" Amy said. She glanced at her watch. "I should go and get ready. We're going to the cemetery at ten-thirty." She looked at Daniel. "Would you like to come?"

He shook his head. "Thanks for asking," he said. "But I wouldn't feel right going."

Amy understood. After all, Daniel hadn't known her mom. "Sure," she said. "Well, I'd better go get changed."

She went upstairs, but as she pulled a formal grey skirt out of her wardrobe, she stopped. *Mom wouldn't want us to dress up*, she thought to herself. *She'd want us to go as we are.* Putting the skirt back in her closet, she pulled on her jeans and went down the corridor to Lou's room.

"I'm not dressing up," she said, as Lou opened her bedroom door.

"Why?" Lou said in surprise.

"Mom wouldn't have wanted it," Amy answered. "She'd want us to be as she remembered."

"Yes," Lou smiled. "I think you're right."

Twenty minutes later, Amy was standing with her friends and family by her mom's grave.

Grandpa said a few words of welcome and then read out the same poem that Amy had read at the memorial ceremony nearly a year ago. As the words filled the air, a breeze lifted Amy's hair, and she remembered the Native American phrase that Huten, a friend of her mom's, had told her not so long ago: *there is no death, only a change of worlds.*

Mom's gone, Amy realized suddenly. *But her spirit lives on. In me — in everything I do.*

Grandpa stopped talking and Amy realized he had finished

the poem. Everyone began to slowly move away.

Grandpa came over to her. "Are you ready to go home now, honey?"

"Can I just have a moment by myself?" Amy asked.

Grandpa placed a kiss on her forehead. "Of course." He went over to Lou, put an arm around her shoulders and they led the way back to the parking lot.

"Will you be all right?" Ty squeezed her hand.

Amy nodded. She waited until she was alone and all was quiet, then she knelt by the grave. "Mom," she whispered. "I think I understand. I've got to use the talents that I have. I'll help any horse, sick or healthy, that comes my way, and I'll ride in shows as well. And who knows — maybe I'll be just like you."

She shut her eyes. The breeze caressed her hair. It was so gentle, she could almost imagine it was her mom's kiss.

After a moment, she opened her eyes and touched the headstone. *The world's changed now that you're gone, Mom*, she thought, *but I know you're with me in whatever I do and I'll carry on your work. I promise.*